Charles Asbury Stephens

# The Young Moose Hunters

A Backwood's Story

Charles Asbury Stephens

**The Young Moose Hunters**
*A Backwood's Story*

ISBN/EAN: 9783744641319

Printed in Europe, USA, Canada, Australia, Japan

Cover: Foto ©Andreas Hilbeck / pixelio.de

More available books at **www.hansebooks.com**

FRED AIMED AT THE BACK OF THE MOOSE'S HEAD. — PAGE 210

# The Young Moose-Hunters

## A Backwood's Story

BY

## C. A. STEPHENS

AUTHOR OF "THE KNOCKABOUT CLUB IN THE WOODS," "THE KNOCKABOUT
CLUB ALONG SHORE," "CAMPING-OUT STORIES," ETC.

FULLY ILLUSTRATED

BOSTON
PUBLISHED BY ESTES AND LAURIAT

# LIST OF ILLUSTRATIONS.

# THE YOUNG MOOSE-HUNTERS.

## CHAPTER I.

### PREPARATION.

MY chum took out three greasy, tattered ten-cent "scrips."
"My whole pile!" said he, smoothing them out on the
bare table-leaf, — "all I've got in the world; and this I owe you,
old fellow." And the writer of this narrative, dejectedly watching
him from the other side of the table, was not in a condition to deny
the debt.

"No matter about it this morning, Scott," I said, with a sense of
magnanimity. "I've got twenty-five cents left yet. Besides, the
Lexicon is mine, you know."

"Yes," said Scott, brightening a little; "that's good for two
dollars, any day."

Then we mused.

A glance at us there, in our forlorn little room, would have told
the reader what we were, — a couple of impoverished youngsters,
students for the time being at the village academy, working every
way to wrest an education from Poverty's grim hands.

Ah! those impecunious, starveling school-days of ours! Thanks
to Providence, and the steady revolution of the earth, they are
gone, — forever, I hope. For one, I have no desire to get them
back.

America, meaning the United States, is a great country for self-made men, so called.  Our people rather dote on that sort of man. It is a nice topic to fire the juvenile mind with, — this being a self-made man.  When the average poor boy comes to try for it, he is apt to find it a stern task.

To fight his way against everything, even hunger itself, is doubtless an indication of pluck, yet is it anything save a pleasant pastime for the luckless youth who gives the indication.

That little upstairs room, with its one window, bare floor, and rusty stove; its two crippled chairs and starved little cupboard, that rarely could show more than half a dry loaf of wheat bread and a pint jug of molasses; its unpainted, uncovered table, on which lay half-a-dozen second-hand text-books of Virgil, Cæsar, Xenophon, all intimately associated with a certain void within the waistband, — well, it is not quite an enjoyable recollection, though a very vivid one.  Those were times that tried not only our souls, but our stomachs as well.  And with youngsters of fifteen or thereabouts, the stomach pleads strongly.

To offset all these mortifications of the flesh, we had before us the grand design of fitting for college, beyond which lay the great glowing future shining with professional honors and the bright aureole of fame.

How many young Americans does ambition thus spur to a long and sometimes fruitless struggle for higher and better things!  Every college in the land is strongly represented by those who could have well understood our case that morning; though I honestly hope there are few who were ever quite so badly off.

Presently the academy bell rang, and we hurried off to recite our sixty lines of Virgil.

But the grave and pressing questions of finance that had obtruded themselves so imperatively upon our attention soon recurred; they were not to be put off.  Rather they had been put off till the last moment already.

"MY WHOLE PILE!" SAID HE.

"Something must be done," said Scott; "right off, too. Here we are, — only fifty-five cents — and that Lexicon."

The Latin Lexicon (Andrews and Stoddard's) I had bought at the opening of the term; five precious hard-earned dollars had gone for it, — five of the twenty-seven in my pocket on the last day of August, earned at sweaty toil, "haying" by the day.

"I suppose I can get a school to teach up in Newry this winter," Scott observed, at length. "I have partly had the promise of it. But the pay is only seventeen dollars a month, and it is but for seven weeks. That would not be worth waiting for."

For my own part, I had not even this resource in view. The most of School Committees would have deemed us too young for pedagogues; and so we were.

Nor was it of any use to go home, — a few miles out of the village. Our friends were not able to assist us. Indeed, if any assisting were done, it must come from us to them.

"We shall have to shoulder our axes and go into the logging-swamp," I exclaimed at last. "No other way. Twenty-five dollars a month and board. It's hard and it's low; but there's nothing else — for us."

"And live in an old lousy shanty all winter long, with a crew of profane, drunken, tobacco-chewing fellows!" groaned Scott. "Such company degrades one. We should come out next spring rough as files, ourselves. I don't like it!"

No more did I; yet we must do something. Scott admitted that there was no other way in which we could earn so much; but he shrank from the companionship of loggers. Before the war, when his father was alive, Scott's family had been in better circumstances. I call him Scott from long habit; his name was Henry Scott Whitman.

All that day we were in perplexity, and studied but idly. The question of the morning preoccupied us.

"Let's go over and talk with Fred," Scott proposed that evening.

Fred Bartlett was a classmate and kindred spirit, in like circumstances: that is to say, he had nothing save what his own hands got for him. Fred was seventeen. His home was in Andover, Maine (one of the northern towns of Oxford County). This was his second term at our academy. He had worked at river-driving, in the logging-swamps, and during the previous summer had been a guide to parties from the city camping out about the Umbagog Lakes. A downright good fellow was Fred, wiry and tough as a rat, and full of a rough worldly wisdom born of hard knocks.

We knew him to be nearly out of funds, and on the verge of some expedient for raising more.

So we went over to talk with Fred.

"What are you going into this fall?" Scott asked, after some preliminary conversation.

"Well," said Fred, "I have about concluded to start up the Magalloway for Parmachenee Lake."

"What doing?" we asked.

"Trapping; and I shall hunt some."

"Ever up there?" Scott inquired.

"No; but I've heard all about it. Good place. I calculate I'm sure of a hundred dollars there."

"You do!" we exclaimed.

"I do," said Fred, confidently. "And then," he added after a pause, "if I don't find mink and otter, why, I'll dig a big pack of spruce-gum; that sells well, now."

"Going alone?" I asked.

"Well, I've nobody engaged for certain."

"But what will you live on up there?" Scott demanded. "What will you do for grub to eat?"

"Oh, I'll find enough to eat. I shall take along some flour and meat. Then there are plenty of deer and moose and trout up there. I'll live like a king, I tell you."

Then we talked of other matters.

At last, as we were going out, Scott said, " I suppose you would n't care to take us along with you, Fred ? "

Fred reflected a moment; then he said that he should like to have us go well enough, if we would like to go.

Yet we presumed he did not care much for our company; in fact, Scott had asked him more in jest than in earnest.

The next morning, however, Fred asked us if we thought of going, and gave us a more cordial invitation.

Then we began to consider the matter more seriously, and, indeed, talked of little else between ourselves for the next two days. It seemed a wild project, yet in want of anything else to do we were much disposed to try it; and at length we told Fred definitely that we would go.

On that, he set the day for us to meet him at Upton, at the foot of Lake Umbagog, and at once started for home to get ready.

Being now fairly in for the expedition, we began to make our own arrangements.

We settled the rent of our bare room for the week, — forty cents.

We sold the Lexicon for two dollars and a half; also a Common School Arithmetic (Greenleaf's), a Smyth's Algebra, and a Cooper's Virgil for three dollars more. (It was no uncommon thing with us in those days to dispose of our books — at ruinous discounts — toward the end of a term.)

I swapped my best (tweed) coat at the store for two old army blankets.

Scott made a similar exchange for two rubber blankets.

It got out that we were going *moose-hunting !* Everybody pooh-poohed at us; and our friends croaked dismally, but in vain.

We bought ammunition, sparingly. Scott had an old double-barrelled gun that had been his father's; and a young sporting-man in the village — whose name I will not needlessly drag into this Iliad of our fortunes — loaned us, by his own offer, a little breech-loading rifle, the skeleton stock of which could be taken off when desired. It was of the pattern popularly known as " The Hunter's Pet." And with it he let us take two boxes of metallic cartridges. This was a windfall, indeed.

Another friend in need gave Scott a pair of rubber boots. Vainly I wished for a similar friend.

By Saturday night of that week we had completed our slender outfit. We were to meet Fred at Upton Monday night or Tuesday morning of the following week.

# CHAPTER II.

WE started at six o'clock Monday morning, October 3, and walked ten miles to "Locke's," a station on the Grand Trunk Railroad. Our packs were heavy; but we were fresh then, and full of vim, — to quote from our late Latin exercises. Bethel was the next point to make, distant five miles; and as it is on the railroad, we concluded to indulge ourselves in the luxury of a twenty-five-cent ride, by way of saving up our strength.

The Canada express-train whistled in, ten minutes after, and was signalled to stop for our benefit, — Locke's not being one of its advertised stations. We took passage for Bethel with our packs and guns, where we arrived fifteen minutes later. From the depot we caught sight of the high wooded mountains of the northern lake region, looming up grandly across the Androscoggin Valley. Adown their long slopes rested the soft autumn haze; and the rich tints of the foliage gave to the whole country a warm, dreamy look, which I recall with a sense of enjoyment, though our minds were intent on more practical matters.

Our next point was Upton, on Lake Umbagog, distant twenty-six miles, where we were to meet Fred with his boat. From Bethel to Upton there is a stage twice a week. This much we had learned, and had come on the right day for it. We had thought the fare would not be more than fifty cents apiece, and were prepared to give that. Judge, then, of our dismay when we were told that the charge was *two dollars and fifty cents per head !* This announcement struck us speechless. We drew back into the depot to take counsel of each other. Meanwhile the stage drove off.

" Well, let it go!" exclaimed Scott, gazing evilly after the departing vehicle. " We never could have afforded it. Two dollars and a half! Only think of it!"

" But what shall we do?" said I, with a despairing glance at our heavy packs.

" Do! why, we 've got old Shank's mare left us!" exclaimed my stout-hearted comrade. " If a fellow has n't money, he must *frog i*; — that 's all."

But to *frog it* twenty-six miles and carry a pack of thirty-five pounds and a gun is a severe experience — for most boys of sixteen. There was now no help for it, however. We summoned up our reso-lution, but first sat down on the wooden settle in the depot and ate a substantial lunch of the crackers and cheese we had taken along with us from home that morning; thereby lightening our packs a little, and stowing the weight where it could be more comfortably carried.

This done we slung the packs across our backs, and taking our guns in our hands, set off. It was rather warm. By the time we had crossed the long covered bridge over the Androscoggin, we were in a lively perspiration, and drew up to take a " rest " in the shade of the farther end of it. There had been a heavy rain a few days previously. The river was high, and had only the day before flooded the road at both ends of the bridge, which is elevated high above the stream to withstand the tremendous spring freshets. The Androscoggin is the outlet of all those northern lakes toward which we had now set our faces. At this place it is near two hundred yards in width, with a swift, black, arrowy current surging against the strong granite piers. In seasons of drought, however, the Androscoggin can sometimes be forded.

It is a pleasant road beyond the bridge. Many well-to-do farmers live along the intervals. Their residences evince good taste and considerable wealth. The hills and slopes, on the west and north of these farms, abound with sugar maples. And all these were now in their autumn glories of red and gold. The folks were getting in their corn, load after load of dry shocks; and as we trudged on, we caught many a glimpse of cosey husking-parties — merry boys and rosy girls — through the open barn doors.

Steeling our hearts against these alluring pictures, we hurried forward, crossed the bridge over Sunday River, — a tributary of the Androscoggin, — and a little later the Bear River bridge, and entered the town of Newry, — a region chiefly noted for its snow squalls, which are said to begin early in September.

The scenery had grown wilder. The mountains seem nearer, higher, and more rugged. The road leads up the narrow valley of Bear River.

But I must not omit a little incident which associated Bear River bridge with that day's tramp. Just across the stream, and at the very entrance to the covered bridge, there is a little weather-beaten tavern that has evidently seen all of its *best* days and the most of its *worst* ones. Everything about it bespoke neglect, decay, and shiftlessness. Our packs oppressed us, and we sat down on the steps of the tavern to take breath. Presently the landlord came out. He was a rather fat, jug-shaped man of sixty, or rising; he smelled of liquor, and was evidently well soaked with it. Yet in the corner of his light-gray eye there dwelt a gleam of good-humor, — a lingering gleam that even the blight of alcohol could not quite kill out. He addressed us cheerily; and it took not many explanations on our part to make him fully understand our case and the hardships before us. And he did not discourage us, as everybody else had done. He chuckled, and told us to " keep a stiff upper lip."

" Oh, you 'll sup sorrow and rue the day you started, a good many times, I 'll warrant ye," he chirped. " But if you stick and hang, you 'll bring back a clever pack o' furs, like 's not."

Then he limped back into the tavern, and soon came out with a pewter pitcher.

"Take a swig o' this," said he. "It'll wash the dust out o' yer throats. Oh, it's nothing but cider!" he exclaimed, seeing us draw back a little; "nothing but elderberry cider. I don't keep anything stronger. Law won't let me. 'T wont hurt ye."

We first tasted it, then took a few swallows. It was a very pleasant drink, — sweet elderberry juice sweetened and lightly fermented; not so thick and strong as elderberry wine, nor yet so smart as apple cider. I suppose the old fellow thought it was the best thing he could offer us; and I am not sure whether it injured our *morale* as Good Templars or not. We thanked him, and shouldered our packs.

"Call when you come back along, if you come this way, and let me know how you've made it," was his parting salutation to us.

"Well, all old drunkards are not monsters; and I suppose that 'most everybody has some good in them somewhere," Scott remarked as we walked on.

Consider it as I will, I never can feel anything but a kindly sympathy for the old soaker who keeps the Bear River tavern, — so powerful is a kind word when a boy is tired and half-discouraged.

We went on up the valley. Off to the west towered the "Sunday River Whitecap;" to the east rose the "Great Ledge," — a bare, rough peak, cone-shaped, and of great height. The river is here a mere torrent, broken by frequent falls, and rushing along a bed full of bowlders and ledges. The road in many places was half washed away by the recent flood; and high up amid the alder branches were lodged grass and leaves, showing to what a height the stream had risen. Often after heavy rains the stage cannot get up for the water. There is no stream in New England more subject to great and marvellously rapid rise.

Still wilder and narrower grew the valley. The dark-green twin peaks of Mt. Saddleback were directly ahead of us; while the loftier side of Speckled Mountain shut us in on the west. A single narrow gorge opened before us.

"This must be 'Grafton Notch,'" said Scott; and so it proved.

There are few localities in New England that for wild scenery can compare with this famous "Notch," through which Bear River foams and roars to its own confused and hollow echoes.

About a mile farther up the gorge we came to a very singular cataract, or rather *cañon*, called "Screw-Auger Falls." It was but a few yards from the road; and we laid down our packs to examine it. An extensive granite ledge fills the whole bottom of the gorge; and through this the stream has worn a mighty auger-shaped channel, which is of itself a curiosity well worth a visit. This miniature cañon is about a hundred feet in length, and so narrow that at some points one can leap across it; while its depth toward the lower end cannot be less than sixty or seventy feet, — a chasm grooved out by the rushing waters, and smooth as if polished with sand-paper. Its vast spirals probably suggested the name of *Screw-Auger.*

Its sides disclose some remarkable veins of white quartz, with which there seem to be intermingled other minerals, which we had not the time to examine; but which we confidentially recommend to mineralogists as well worth their notice.

As an example of the wearing power of running water, these falls are indeed remarkable.

"There's a good ten thousand years' work!" exclaimed Scott, peeping cautiously down the chasm. "The water did n't wear this hole in one century, nor five!"

It was now four o'clock, and the sun had already gone behind the great mountain on the other side of the stream. There is a little shed on the side of the road opposite the falls, where teams have been hitched up to rest.

"We might put up here for the night," Scott suggested.

But we concluded to go on.

A little way beyond the falls another curiosity drew our attention. On the very verge of the road, though half hidden by the shrubbery, there is a semi-circular abyss known locally as " The Jail," from the fact that there is but one way into it, which, if secured, might make it possible to use it as a place of confinement. The sides are smooth and of great height. It would be quite impossible to climb out. Formerly the river ran through it for many ages, till it wore this great cavity. But an earthquake, or perhaps its own wearing waters, have now given it a new channel some rods to the westward.

After a peep at the Jail, we went on again for a mile or more, till, coming to where some belated wanderers like ourselves, perhaps, had made a little bark shed near the road, we decided to camp for the night. The shed had not been used of late; but the old shake-down of hemlock boughs lay just as its former occupants had left it. It felt dry, and to our tired bodies, looked inviting. Near by stood the flayed hemlocks, from whose trunks the bark had been stripped to furnish the roof of the shed. While I unpacked the blankets, and counted out five crackers apiece for our supper, Scott gathered sticks and pulled bark from a neighboring white birch. Three smutty stones and several old brands marked the place where our predecessors had built their fire. We followed their example, and soon had a crackling blaze. Ah! what so cheery, when twilight and the wilderness are about one, as the red gleam and cheerful snapping of a camp fire! Blessings on the man who struck the first spark of fire, — be he Prometheus or ugly old Vulcan!

In the light of our fire, which gleamed brighter as dusk fell, we ate our crackers and cheese, then gathered, ere darkness closed in, several armfuls of wood to last through the night. The stars came out. The night was clear, with the suggestion of a frost. A very small new moon showed itself for a few minutes on the wooded crest of the mountain, then went behind it, leaving it not perceptibly darker.

WE SOON HAD A CRACKLING BLAZE.

We sat beneath the shed and watched the sparks darting up, and the slower wreath of black smoke rising toward the stars, momentarily clouding their silver sparkle.

Just then the cry of some animal was heard from the mountain side above us. It was not loud nor startling, but a lonely cry of discontent or hunger. Such sounds impress one strangely in the forest at night. We listened to hear it again, and soon it resounded anew; rather more distinctly this time, or else it was because we were hearkening with intent ears.

"Do you know what that is?" Scott asked.

I could not even guess. It is often very difficult to identify animal cries heard in the woods at night-time. The forest echoes change the character of the note. This sounded somewhat like a man shouting rather disconsolately at a distance. We continued to hear it, at intervals of ten or fifteen minutes. But it did not alarm us much. We gradually grew sleepy.

"Had we best both go to sleep?" queried Scott.

It did not seem just right to do so.

"Tell you what we will do," said Scott, at length. "You roll up and go to sleep. I'll take the little rifle, and sit leaned back against the side of the shed. I won't go to sleep; but I can sit and doze till one or two o'clock. Then I will wake you, and you can take your turn at it. It will rest a fellow almost as much to sit so as it would to lie down."

I had nothing to urge against this arrangement, and was, in truth, very glad to get the first nap. We had walked, carrying our packs, not less than twenty-four miles that day. So utterly weary had I become, that I wrapped my two blankets about me, and despite the novelty of the situation, was soundly asleep in less than fifteen minutes.

# CHAPTER III.

## IN CAMP.

WHATEVER went on about our camp, and what savage eyes may have stared at us lying there as the stars moved westward and set behind the mountain wall, is no part of my story. When I woke it was broad daylight. Indeed, the sun-rays had begun to glint the tree-tops. So profoundly had I been asleep that it was several seconds before I knew "who I was or where I came from." Scott was half sitting, half reclining, against one of the stakes that supported the shed, his head rolled on one shoulder, and his mouth open, sound asleep. The little rifle had slid from his grasp, and lay with the dewdrops clinging to the muzzle. The fire had long gone out. It did not even smoke. Outside, the ground and the grass in the road were frosty. I got upon my feet, feeling pretty stiff and not a little chilly. Then I gave my recusant comrade a poke, — several of them. He started with a great groan of discomfort. It was with difficulty that he got his neck out of the unnatural position it had held for so many hours.

"You're a nice fellow to keep guard!" I exclaimed.

Scott winked painfully.

"I suppose I must have got to sleep," said he, staring at his legs and at the dewy rifle.

It looked like it.

"But why did n't you wake me?" said he.

"Why did n't I wake you!" I indignantly repeated. "That's a pretty question for a sentinel to ask!"

"Well, as long as we're all right this morning, there's no great harm done," was my comrade's philosophic reflection.

I was not for letting him off so easily, but contented myself by remarking that this sort of thing must not happen again.

We did not think it worth while to rekindle the fire, it had got so late, — how late we were uncertain, for Scott had forgotten to wind his watch the night before; it had run down. We had eight crackers left, and the rinds of the cheese. Hastily devouring these refreshments, we took a hearty draught from a little rill which ran across a ledge a few rods away, then rolled up our packs and went on.

In a few minutes we were in the narrowest part of the Notch; and though we were not at all poetically disposed this morning, yet the grandeur of the scenery compelled us to pause frequently to gaze up at the overhanging cliffs and crags. Bear River, now dwindled to a noisy brook, brawls and murmurs hoarsely along the ravine. The road crosses the stream as many as six times; the bridges are of logs, covered with hemlock boughs and earth. At one point the road is made along the side of the gorge, which sinks to a great depth below. The only railing beside the wagon-track is a log.

"Shouldn't care to drive a skittish horse here," was Scott's practical observation, as we looked into the abyss beneath. To which I recollect replying that I only wished we had a horse to drive; for the packs were growing fearfully heavy again.

Near this place there is another wonderful exhibition of the wear of the water through a ledge. It is known as "Moose Caves," from the circumstance of a wounded moose once taking refuge in the cavern which the stream has worn. Those with whom I have spoken concerning it say that it is more wonderful than Screw-Auger Falls even. It is at some little distance from the road; we did not go out to it.

A mile farther on the road emerges from the Notch, disclosing a less mountainous country to the northward, heavily wooded with evergreens chiefly. The ground here begins to descend toward the

Umbagog. Near by are the headwaters of a stream which, oddly enough, some settler has named Cambridge River. There are clearings along the road. On one of the barn-doors we saw a fresh bearskin, stretched and nailed to dry. Scott wanted to shoot at it, but was deterred by the suggestion that there might be somebody husking in the barn.

We were now in the town of Grafton.

We followed the "Cambridge" down as we had followed Bear River up, and about one o'clock came in sight of the blue Umbagog, stretching away to the northwest. Before us a long hill led down to the white "Lake House," which we espied on the very shore. The sight of it gave us new life. We re-shouldered our packs and hurried down the hill. A hundred rods from the tavern we saw two young fellows and a dog coming to meet us.

"That's Fred, — one of them!" Scott exclaimed.

There was no doubt of it, for a moment later that worthy young backwoodsman gave us his ordinary salutation. "Money!" he shouted, presenting an imaginary revolver. "Hands up! Drop that rifle!"

"You're badly sold this time!" replied Scott. "If money's what you're after, you've stopped the wrong party."

That was but a grim joke, — too true to be pleasant.

"We will have some money, though, if there is any fur round these lakes!" cried Fred. "But why in the world did n't you come last night? Looked for you till eight o'clock in the evening. Thought that catamount down in the Notch had got you, sure!"

"That what?" said I.

"Why, that catamount down there! Have n't you heard about him?"

Certainly we had not! Scott looked rather uneasily at me. Then I told them how we had camped there in the Notch, and both slept like logs.

"MONEY!" HE SHOUTED, PRESENTING AN IMAGINARY REVOLVER.

"Well, well!" exclaimed Fred, and laughed heartily. "It's a wonder he had not gobbled you up! Folks don't dare go through there nights, lately."

"Is that true?" exclaimed Scott.

"Honest true. But no matter, as long as he did n't get ye. This long-legged chap here" (with a nod toward the stranger youth) "is going into partnership with us. His name is Farr, — Charles Henry Farr; and this quadruped is his dog. Come here, Spot! He is n't worth anything for small game, but he is good for chewing up panthers, lions, bears, and bug-bears."

Farr was a rather tall, frank-faced fellow of seventeen or thereabouts. We liked him at sight; and if the reader does not, it will be our fault, not his. As for Spot, he was an average-sized dog, black and white. He appeared remarkably inoffensive, and did not look like a dog addicted to "chewing up" anything livelier than a crust of bread.

"We shall not be able to get started up the lake to-day," said Fred. "But let's go to the house; you must be hungry and tired."

He and Farr seized upon our packs. It was a relief to walk without their weight.

Landlord Godwin, of the Lake House, is as good a host, at bottom, as lives in that whole region. It takes a day to get fairly acquainted with him. He has a way of hesitating when he speaks that makes a stranger feel a little uncertain for a moment. But when you once come to know him, you know a good fellow, — in our humble opinion. His table is a very enjoyable one. (A person is always hungry up there.) That day we dined off the breasts of six partridges; there were other eatables, of course, but the partridges were the attraction for us. Perhaps I am hasty, though, in saying that the birds were the attraction for all of us. For a certain black-eyed, raven-tressed table-girl took Scott's eyes captive. During our stay

there he managed to get up a speaking acquaintance with her.
Afterwards he seemed to be somewhat distressed to learn that this
siren of the lakes had a " young man " whom she kept happy company
of a Saturday eve: one Llewellyn Moody, a youthful Atlas of the
region, with whom it would be advisable to remain on the most civil
terms.

Fred and Farr had brought with them and bought of Godwin
all the raw provisions that they deemed necessary, together with a
complete kit of camping-out utensils.

A complete kit of camping-out comfortably embraces more than
would at first thought be deemed necessary. We had, I remember,
a kettle for making pudding and baking beans; a kettle for heating
water; a deep frying-pan or spider with a very long handle, — three
feet, — such as can be used over an open fire without burning the
hands; and a large iron baker-sheet for cooking partridge breasts and
biscuits. Then there was a coffee-pot and a teapot, half-a-dozen tin
plates, as many pint dippers, four tin spoons, with the same number
of knives and forks, a hatchet, and an axe. There were also two
butcher knives for cutting meat, — one a sort of bowie-knife with a dog's
head handle, loaned us by Godwin. Add to these an old japanned tin
powder-case for the sugar, a bucket for butter, a tin box for coffee, and
another for the tea.

In addition to all this " kitchen ware " were the two rubber
blankets and the two wool blankets, and an old " puff " that Farr
had brought; also an A tent, seven by seven, that is, seven feet square
on the ground.

Some of these articles might, perhaps, have been dispensed with ;
yet the most of them were really necessary. And on account of this
amount of necessary luggage it is better for a party — whether going
for pleasure or otherwise — to go as much by water as possible, in a
good, roomy boat.

An account was kept of everything bought, so that in the end each could pay his proportionate part of the expenses; this was what we had agreed upon at the outset. Fred's boat, in which they had already stowed all the luggage, lay in the river a few rods from the house. It was a sort of bateau, about twenty-four feet long by four feet in width amidships. Once it had been painted white with a red lapstreak, but hard service and stormy waters had much defaced it.

Fred had brought with him two dozen of traps, and Farr had a dozen. Of guns we had a great supply, — more guns than ammunition, as it turned out. Fred had a long single-barrelled shot-gun, and Farr had a double-barrelled shot-gun and a Sharpe's army (cavalry) carbine, one of those clumsy breech-loaders in which the barrel is connected and held to the chamber by an iron strap in front of the trigger guard. In loading, this strap acts as a lever to slide the barrel forward from the chamber, into which it fits rather loosely. The chamber is then filled with powder, and the bullet is thrust into the base of the barrel. The strap is then snapped into position, bringing the barrel with the ball down against the chamber and the powder. A percussion cap is then placed upon a nipple and tube entering the chamber, and the piece is ready for firing. All these weapons besides our own!

For provisions Fred had got a sack of flour, some pork, a half bushel of corn meal, a bushel of potatoes, three pounds of coffee, a pound of tea, four pounds of sugar, a quantity of butter, and two papers of Horsford's " Bread Preparation," — this last for making warm biscuits.

In the little garden attached to the Lake House there was a thicket of plum-trees, of the kind called "Canada Plums," similar to pomegranates. To these we helped ourselves liberally; for they grew in liberal quantities. The ground beneath the shrubs was literally red with the plums. Everybody ate all they wanted, — and no questions.

# CHAPTER IV.

A S soon as it was fairly light next morning, we were astir. Breakfast was eaten. Godwin's bill against us was a very light one.
He charged us not half the usual hotel rates. It was well he did not,
or we should have been utterly bankrupted then and there.

Some minutes before sunrise we went aboard our boat and took our
places for the long pull up the lakes. There were two sets of row-locks,
with oars to match. Fred took one pair and Farr the other. Spot
lay down on Farr's coat behind his master. I took the stern seat
and steering oar. Scott had the bow seat and a paddle.

"All ready!" cried Fred, cheerily. "Give way! One, two, three,
and away we go!"

Following the crooked channel of the Cambridge, it is nearly a
mile out to the lake proper; yet when the gates are down at Errol,
the Umbagog flows back to the very yard fence at Godwin's. The
flats were now in part overflowed. The morning had been clear and
calm; but directly after sunrise the wind began to blow from the
southwest. By the time we were fairly out of the Cambridge on the
lake, there was quite a "sea."

Fred kept glancing uneasily at the sky.

"No danger, is there?" said Scott.

"No danger here," replied Fred. "But if this wind keeps rising,
we shall have it rough up toward the Narrows!"

This prediction rather dampened the jolly spirits in which we
had embarked. We grew less talkative, but rowed the harder. A

few minutes later we rounded B. Point and saw the whole southern half of the lake before us. Rather rough and windy it looked, too.

"No white caps yet!" said Farr, turning on his seat for a look ahead. "Guess we can go through, Fred."

"Can't tell that yet," said Fred. "It's a thing you can't count on, — this lake. Gets up quicker than Jack-in-a-box if a puff of wind blows. My opinion is, if we want to get through those Narrows this forenoon we have no time to lose."

On this hint we all began pulling with a will. To avoid the trough of the waves, we kept the boat headed northwest till we were within three fourths of a mile of the west shore, then turned her squarely to the northeast, with the wind at our backs, and heading straight into the Narrows, four miles distant.

For the first ten minutes we rode as lightly as a duck, and shot ahead rapidly. The boat was not heavily loaded for its size. But soon white caps began to show, and the swells grew larger. The boat began to bounce on them and the spatters to fly. We kept steadily at our work, however, and under our united strength the bateau went about as fast as the waves, though a few big swells combed into the stern, making my seat far from comfortable.

Ten minutes more, and we were within a mile of the Narrows. All about, the waves were running white. The boat was plunging heavily. The spray flew in upon us. The roar of the dashing was so great that we could scarcely hear each others' voices. Spot howled dismally. I confess to being considerably scared; for the wind blew smartly, and all down through the Narrows the lake was as rough as a cataract. Just then Scott's hat flew off and was dashed out of sight several rods ahead.

"Never mind that!" he shouted. "Let it go! I've got an old cap in my pack."

"Steady!" shouted Fred. "Hold her steady, Farr!"

Then he turned for a look. We were bouncing prodigiously.

" I fear for her backbone ! " groaned Scott.

" Take a look, Farr, and tell me what you think of it," said Fred, resuming his oars.

Farr looked.

" Never saw it worse," said he. " I don't know, but I 'm afraid it will be too much for her. I should say, go for Birch Island."

" Birch Island it is, then ! " exclaimed Fred. " Head her for that island off to the right of us ! " he added to me, pointing to where a clump of white birches and a few evergreens seemed to rise out of the waves about a hundred rods away.

I had all I could do to hold the boat steady with the steering oar. The swells threw us about amazingly. There is a strength and friskiness in these fresh-water surges that is never felt on the more staid salt water. Those were wild moments. Fred, Farr, and Scott were pulling with might and main. The spray flew over us; the spatters drenched us. I expected every moment that we should be swamped. And as we drew near the island, our case seemed not much improved. The waves broke against it fiercely.

" It won't do to let her run on there ! " exclaimed Farr. " It will stave her ! "

" Yes," said Fred. " But it is not deep water. Sit still and pull till I give the word, then jump out everybody, and ease her ashore."

" Now for it ! Over with you ! " he shouted, a moment afterwards.

We leaped out, and carried the boat by main strength high upon the sand.

It had been a sharp tussle. Never was I so glad to set my foot on firm earth. We were drenched to our skins. The rubber coats and blankets had protected the flour and meal and sugar; but everything else was soaked, and the boat was a third full of water. The wind, piercing our wet clothes, made us shiver despite the exertion. As soon as we could secure the boat we ran to the lee of the birch and cedar thicket that occupied the middle of the islet.

"NOW FOR IT! OVER WITH YOU!"

"Let's have a fire and dry ourselves," exclaimed Scott. "We shall have to stay here till the wind lulls."

Farr got the axe from the boat, and fell to splitting up dry cedar; a rather large cedar (for the island) had blown down some years before, and now lay dry and broken among large stones. He soon had a great pile of it split.

"Who's got a match?" he cried.

Scott took out his little tin match-box and opened it, but stopped short with a loud exclamation, —

"Wet! — every one wet as a sop!" And he poured water out of the box.

Fred laughed. "Let me see if my match-box is as bad off as yours."

He pulled out a flat bottle tightly corked.

"This is my match-box," said he. "Takes more than one soaking to wet that — inside."

And his were the only matches that had escaped.

We soon had a fire going, — a rousing one, about which we stood and steamed in the shelter of the thicket. The roar of the agitated lake came to our ears from the windward side of the islet; but on the lee side the water was not very rough. Up at the Narrows it looked white and tumultuous; and against the rocky side of Metallic Island, half a mile above, we could see the surf leap up eight and ten feet, white as milk. I vowed inwardly not to put out on the lake again till the wind went down, if I had to stay there alone two weeks. Farr kept asking us how we should like to be "out there now," — pointing toward the weltering Narrows.

We began to feel like having dinner. Fred brought round the frying-pan and a piece of pork. This was cut into slices, and "sizzled" in the pan. The fat looked very clear and good. At home neither Scott nor I ate salted pork, or the fat. But when Fred brought round a dozen crackers, and Farr had made a pot of strong tea, we felt a good appetite to sit down round the "spider," each with a fork to break and dip pieces of cracker in the fat and sip dippers of sweet tea without milk.  We seemed to need the fat after our drenching.

"I begin to understand how the Esquimaux can drink train-oil,' remarked Scott.  "It's the cold and the rough life they lead that makes it relish."

The wind continued to blow all through the middle of the day. It always does here, when once it gets started.  We began to think we should have to spend the night on the island; but toward four o'clock, afternoon, it subsided considerably, and the swells fell with it.

"Let's start," said Fred.  "We can get as far as Moll's Rock, and have time to camp before dark."

We bailed out the boat, then got in and pushed off.

"What's 'Moll's Rock'?" inquired Scott.

"It is a ledge on the west shore about a mile below the outlet" (Androscoggin), Farr explained.  "They call it Moll's Rock, from old Mollocket, an Indian squaw, who used to live there.  She had a wigwam on the ledge, a little up from the water, for a good many years. It's a pretty place.  Old Metallic was her husband, it is said.  He was a chief.  That is where they get the name of Metallic Island — from him."

From Birch Island to Moll's Rock it is not far from three miles, as I judged.  The upper portion of Lake Umbagog — the part above the Narrows — is by far the most picturesque.  All about the northern and western sides there are fine bold peaks, with dense unbroken forests, clothing their slopes to the very shores.  The red and gold of the birches and maples was contrasted finely with the black green of the spruce thickets.  A pleasanter scene can hardly be imagined than when the bright glow of the setting sun rested warmly on all this autumnal splendor, and on the broad lake, now quiet as a mirror.  It seems incredible how soon this tumultuous white-capped expanse sinks to repose when the wind falls.  Its calms succeed as rapidly as its bursts of wave-lashed wrath.

Just as the last rays of sunset were burnishing the waters, we pulled into the little cove to the south of Moll's Rock. This is a favorite camping-place for sportsmen on these waters. The place was strewn with the débris of broken boxes, tin cans, and, I regret to say, broken bottles. One bit of board nailed to a tree said that "Warren Noyes and party camped here eleven days, from September 25, 18—, till October 7;" another, driven into the ground like a headstone, informed the passer that thereunder rested the bodies of one hundred and fifty-six ducks, being the surplus above table-use shot by the above party.

We kindled a fire in a stone fireplace built by former occupants, and pitched our tent. Fred got out the "Horsford" and proceeded to knead up a batch of biscuits, using a piece of butter for "shortening." Scott undertook to make tea; and it was my duty to prepare coals and roast for the party two potatoes apiece and one for Spot.

While we were thus engaged, a flock of black ducks went whirring over, flying very low. Farr, who was standing by, seized his shot-gun and let both barrels go among them; and he had the good fortune to *wing* one of them. It fell into the lake at a hundred yards or less from the shore. Farr immediately pushed off to pick it up. But it swam and dived so expertly that he was obliged to shoot it again with Fred's long-barrelled gun. It was a fine large bird, and would have weighed eight pounds, we thought. Farr dressed it and put it on to parboil for breakfast. Fred cut armful after armful of boughs, and made a very comfortable bed inside the tent. On this we spread our rubber blankets and then rolled ourselves up in our wool blankets. The flap of the tent, on the end next the fire, was pinned back to let in the cheerful glow. We lay and talked a long time, planning what we should do when we reached Parmachenee and got into the wild region to the north of it.

Ah! we little knew what was before us, or how many hardships and perils must be braved before we should see Moll's Rock again! Loons with their plaintive wild voices sang us to sleep.

# CHAPTER V.

## ON THE ANDROSCOGGIN.

SCOTT woke the rest of us sometime before sunrise by firing at a loon sailing near, with the little rifle. It startled us rather suddenly; but it was high time we were up. The fire was rekindled. Fred made fritters ("flippers," he called them) out of flour, using some of the bread preparation, and stirring them thinner than for biscuit. Farr finished cooking his duck. I boiled potatoes; and Fred made coffee, — the first we had.

We hurried things, and had breakfast ready a few minutes after sun-peep. And we ate as speedily as possible, for the wind began to blow a little, rising with the sun. We had a mile and a half to go before getting into the outlet; and we did not relish the thought of being cooped up there all day again. Twenty-four hours had passed since we left Godwin's, and we were still only eight miles above the Lake House. From Upton to the head of Lake Parmachenee it is eighty miles. It would take us ten days to get up there, at our first day's rate. We all chafed under this estimate.

"But we will do better to-day," said Fred. "The wind can't swamp us on the river."

"We shall have the current to row against after we get into the Magalloway," suggested Farr; "and a pretty strong old current, too, after all these rains."

Persons do not usually perceive the full magnitude of an enterprise until after they have entered upon it; that was our case, at least.

Spot had what was left of the duck. We struck our tent and

packed up without loss of time. In less than an hour we were embarking again; and an hour is quick time to get breakfast, eat it, and break camp. They who have tried it will say so.

Though the wind had risen considerably, we had no trouble in crossing to the outlet. Off Reed Point the swells made the boat bounce a little; but immediately on making the Point we were in smooth water, and at once pulled into the river.

The Androscoggin, where it first leaves the lake, is very crooked, winding about through a shrubby, alluvial meadow of its own making. It is not more than fifty or sixty yards wide here on an average, with a sluggish and hardly perceptible current.

We passed, hereabouts, what Fred called the headworks of a raft of logs, — itself a raft, upon which was planted a capstan for pulling the greater raft to which it may be attached. It lay high and dry on the bank. About it were scattered heavy levers, capstan-bars, and "thorough shots," — just as the last gang of drivers had abandoned it.

Going on, we entered among a heavy growth of maple and elm, dead and half-fallen.

"The big dam at Errol did it," Fred explained. "Water rose over the roots and killed the trees."

From the place where the Androscoggin leaves the lake to the mouth of the Magalloway, it is about two miles. The latter comes in at nearly right angles from the north. We reached the forks at half-past eight precisely, and at once turned our prow up the stream, toward Parmachenee. Hitherto we had gone with the current, now we had to breast it. For several miles, however, this current is hardly noticeable. At the confluence, the Magalloway looks to be as large as the Androscoggin, and is very deep. Ducks rose in flocks ahead of us and went smartly off up stream.

"This is about as far as I have ever been," Fred remarked. "I have been out here to the mouth of the Magalloway twice, but never any farther. It will be new territory now for the whole of us."

"Well, all we shall have to do will be to follow the river," said Farr. "The stream leads up to the lake; and we cannot very well lose the stream."

Flock after flock of sheldrakes rose one after the other. It was agreed that Scott should ship his paddle and sit in the bow, with the guns cocked and ready for them.

The shores were wooded almost exclusively with firs; the stream was eight and nine rods wide, very dark, and seemingly very deep. About half an hour after entering it, we passed a great swamp on the west bank, which the overflowing waters had now changed to a pond. Here at some distance we saw fully fifty black ducks sailing and splashing about. They were too far off to hit with shot; we did not care to turn the boat into the swamp among the many snags and roots. Scott sent a slug from the rifle skipping among them, at which twenty-five or thirty rose with a great spattering and whirring of wings.

Captain Perkins, of the little lake steamer "Diamond," at Upton, had told Fred to be sure to try Bottle Brook Pond for ducks, going up; and he described the place where we should need to land to go to it so well that we had no trouble in recognizing it. It was about three miles above the mouth of the Magalloway.

The guns were reloaded and plentifully shotted. The secret of shooting well with a shot-gun is to put in a good lot of shot. If you put in a whole handful, they will be pretty sure to knock over something. Bottle Brook Pond lies abreast of the river, from which it is separated by a bank not more than ten feet above high water, and twelve or fifteen rods in width. But this bank is so densely wooded with firs that no glimpse of the pond is obtained from the stream. The pond itself is of no great extent, — eight or ten acres, perhaps.

Carefully securing our boat to a root in the bank, we landed, guns in hand, and cautiously made our way through the firs. Farr, in order to have all the available shooting power ready, had made an experiment, — one he will not care to try again, I fancy: he loaded

IT MADE A TREMENDOUS REPORT.

his Sharpe's *carbine with shot;* pretty heavily, too, it would seem. At any rate, he admitted afterward that he had put in a "good dose" of shot, and powder enough to *a little more than fill the chamber!*

Perkins had predicted rightly. Our first glimpse of the pond through the firs showed it to be alive with both black ducks and sheldrakes. There they were, paddling about, diving, flapping, and spattering the water, with an occasional low quack. The sight of them so near made Scott fairly wild with excitement.

"More than five hundred of them!" he muttered. "We will have them, sure!"

Not daring to disclose ourselves, we crouched under cover of a fallen fir-top, ten or fifteen yards back from the water, amid the shrubbery. We could see them plainly enough, but they had not espied us. It was fun to watch them at play. They were not more than twenty yards from the shore, — not a hundred feet from where we lay in ambush.

They were darting first one way, then another, on the water, but mainly in little groups of three, four, and five together.

"We'll just everlastingly pepper 'em!" whispered Farr. "Five guns — seven barrels. Get good aim, now, and when I count three, blaze away! Ready, now, one — two — three!"

*Whang — bang — whang!* went six barrels.

There was a great smoke, followed by loud quackings of alarm and terror from the pond, and involuntary shouts from the whole of us; Spot barking loudly.

Farr leaped up with the carbine for another shot. Through the smoke we could see the air black with ducks going up off the water with a mighty flutter and rumble of wings. Farr aimed into the flock and fired the carbine. It made a tremendous report, and I saw him reel backward against a tree. The piece itself jumped out of his hands, as if thrown. Farr recovered his legs, but began to shake his hand.

" Hurt ye?" we cried out to him.   " Did it burst?"

" Oh-h-h — ah-h-h !" moaned the carbiner, dancing about.   " It — it — just burst my forefinger !!"

Fred ran to pick up the exploded weapon.   The iron strap had burst, throwing the barrel and chamber apart at full stretch!   It was this broken strap that struck his finger, bruising it badly.   The tube, too, had *spit* the powder and spattered his other hand, burning it slightly.

Leaving him to shake the agonies out of his aching finger, the rest of us turned our attention to the pond.   One duck was splashing about close in to the shore; another lay still on the water a little farther out; and far over on the other side of the pond we could see still another fluttering near the shore.

" Three down !" cried Fred.   " Not so very bad, though we might have done better."

The one near the shore was immediately secured.   But we could not reach the other, and tried in vain to make Spot go in after it. No use.   All he would do was to put his tail betwixt his legs and slink off: he was n't a water-dog.   Finally, by going back to the boat for the hatchet and cutting a very long pole, we contrived to pull in the second one.

Meanwhile Scott and Fred had gone round the pond after the third duck, which they knocked over with a pole and secured without much difficulty.   Thus closed our first duck-shooting exploit.   We were greatly elated — except Farr.   We had three ducks, a shattered gun, and a shattered finger.

# CHAPTER VI.

## THE CROOKED MAGALLOWAY.

THE most crooked stream in the world is the Magalloway. There are crooks about which one may pull a boat two miles without getting ahead twenty rods. At one place, which we reached an hour later, the river is "three double;" so that really we had to row past a given point three times to get by it for good.

We presently emerged from the fir forest into clearings. Here and there a low, weathered house or barn disclosed itself. This is what is known as the Lower Settlement of Magalloway. It is in the edge of New Hampshire. The district is called, on the map, Wentworth's Location. It is not a town, nor yet a plantation. How the people stand related to the great body politic generally, I am sure I don't know. But however their political situation may determine, it must be a blessed nice one, for they have no taxes to pay, — not even poll-tax or school-tax; and yet they have a school, thanks to the State Treasury; for we presently passed a house a little up from the bank, where during the noon recess fifteen or twenty children were disporting.

"Too many for one family," commented Fred. "This must be the place where they have their school."

It looked like that. And there was the schoolmistress (it could be none else) standing in the door. Having a great respect for education, Scott raised his hat to her. She frowned; and being of a dark complexion, the effect was so depressing that we redoubled our efforts and made off without loss of time.

The clearings and cots are on both sides of the river. There are no bridges. In winter (which means eight months of the year here) the folks cross on the ice. In summer they wade it. In spring and fall and after heavy showers they swim it.

A little farther up we passed a two-story house with very comfortable out-buildings. There were also two large bateaux moored to the bank. This is "Spencer's," the headquarters of the Berlin Mills (N. H.) Lumbering Company. Here one may spend the night, or a week if desirable, and have good board at two dollars per day. Tourists now and then get up as far as this place. There is fine trout fishing at Escohos Falls, five or six miles above this point.

Shortly after passing Spencer's, we espied two maidens at a place where a cart track led down the bank to the water — in wading time. They were waiting and casting wistful looks toward the opposite bank. Evidently they wished to get across. There was no boat. They were very pretty girls — from where we were. Fred hailed them politely and asked if they would like to have us set them across in our boat. They regarded us thoughtfully a moment, then precipitately retired into a sweet elder-bush. Modest. But it hurts one's feelings to have well-meant offers received in that way. Again we plied our oars.

Off to the west Mount Dustin, with dark slopes of spruce, walled in the river valley. Due north the great round white peak of Escohos — one of the highest mountains in Maine — rises almost to the snow-line. To the northwest the "Diamond Peaks" display their brown rectangular crags, disclosing a wild, narrow valley, down which comes the swift Diamond stream. The valley resounds to the roar of its cascades. It joins the Magalloway at this place.

A little above the forks, the Magalloway bends from the base of a high hill covered with poplars and white birches. Here we found a strong current. Fred stopped rowing.

" Is n't it getting about time for grub ? " he demanded.

" One o'clock," said Scott, looking at his time-keeper.

"I move we land and get up a dinner," said Farr.

We all felt that way. The boat was laid alongside the bank and made fast to a birch. We jumped ashore, glad to stretch our legs. They felt badly kinked after sitting so long.

We had not taken half-a-dozen steps before a fine birch-partridge flew up to the limb of a poplar.

"Pass the gun, Farr," said Scott, — "the double-barrelled one."

It was handed to him. He fired. Down dropped the bird. But at the report there flew up another from the ground near by and alighted on one of the lowest limbs of a neighboring fir. There it stood motionless, close up to the trunk.

Scott discharged the other barrel, and secured her.

The first one was as large a cock partridge as I had ever seen.

"Looks as if we no need to starve," said Fred. "Three ducks and two partridges the first half day on the river."

Near by were the ruins of an old logging-camp, — a rude structure, consisting of a frame of stakes and poles covered with broad "shingles" of hemlock bark. It was nearly forty feet long by twenty in breadth. Heavy snows, accumulating on the roof, had broken it in. This furnished us fuel. The dry bark burned readily. Nothing, save coal, makes a hotter fire than dry hemlock bark.

Fred set up a "spunhungen," — a pole with one end stuck in the ground and extending out over the fire (an Indian device, hence called by the Indian name), — and soon had potatoes boiling and meat sizzling.

Farr meantime had fallen upon the partridges, and was making the feathers fly like a goshawk. Very soon two plump breasts were in the frying-pan, which was filled partially with water. His way of cooking birds was to first parboil them a few minutes, — or a few hours, as time permitted, — then brown them in the same pan, and make a gravy of flour.

The breast of a partridge is the only part worth eating, in my opinion. We came to eat nothing but those white breasts. The remaining parts we threw to Spot, raw. Unless we were unusually hungry, a breast apiece would be about what we wanted; and unless we had four birds, it was hardly worth while to have a partridge dinner.

In twenty-five minutes after Farr began to pick them, he announced them "done;" and indeed they tasted very well, though Scott pronounced them "a bit too rare."

We stopped an hour here. Considering the fact that we shot, dressed, and cooked our dinner, it was not a long halt. From the circumstances, we named the place Partridge Bluff.

Just as we were embarking, a large flock of ducks came *humming* down the stream. There was a scramble for the guns. Fred fired among them; but they had got a little past. None of them stopped with us.

The current was more rapid, on turning the bend beyond the bluff. We had to work steadily to make fair progress against it, — two miles an hour.

A second flock of ducks went up from the water a few rods above the bend. Scott let two barrels go among them. One tumbled back.

"Good shot!" we shouted.

But the wounded duck dived next moment; and though we waited and watched five or ten minutes, we saw nothing more of it. Possibly it got entangled in the brush beneath the bank, under water, and being severely wounded, drowned there and never rose. Or it may have swum to some distance, and just raising its head above water under cover of some bush or bunch of grass, thus eluded our notice. Old sportsmen tell many stories of the cunning displayed by ducks when too severely wounded to fly off.

There were occasional clearings and old camps along the banks, where lumbering operations had been previously carried on, but no cultivated clearings for a space of six or seven miles above the Lower

Settlement. The current for this whole distance is disagreeably strong, to a party going up. It was not till toward sunset that we sighted an open field and a barn on the left bank, at the foot of a very dark, steep mountain. But long before getting up abreast the building, we struck a current so swift and strong that our former experiences of it were at once belittled. The river curved sharply to the right, disclosing a visible incline, down which the water poured with a steady sweep, swift, black, and arrowy. Several rocks rose above the surface. About these the divided current foamed and threw up white jets. There was a very perceptible roar. Both banks are rather steep, and densely packed with black alders, rendering it wellnigh impossible to land a line to tow with. At the end of our long day it looked disheartening enough. And yet we did not like the idea of camping below it, and having it before us for next day.

For as much as ten minutes we hung in the eddy at the foot of the rapid and studied it, — how to get up best. Fred thought we had better take the mid-channel, where there was ample room between the rocks. We all drew breath, spat on our hands, set our teeth, and at the word from Fred, went at it with a will and under a full head of muscle. The bateau shot out of the eddy, cut into the strong water, and went up, yard after yard, through it, but kept going slower and slower as we drew toward the top.

" We 're gaining!" Fred shouted. " We shall do it!"

We struck quick and with all our strength. So strong was the impulse and so great the resistance of the current, that the boat settled into it almost to the gunwales. Still we gained, inch by inch, and were within ten yards of the top; there we came to a standstill.

" Harder! we 're not gaining!" Fred yelled, panting and buckling to his oars. " Harder! harder!"

" Harder! faster! or we shall go on the rocks!"

Every nerve now! But we could not gain. The mighty strength of the current held us stark and stiff. We sprang and struck and surged with might and main. The water rose round us and roared at us or seemed to. It overmatched us.

"We're losing!" Fred cried out.

Inch by inch we lost a yard, then by a strong spurt retained it, but could not get a foot higher. Our strength was out of us quite. Farr and Scott both stopped pulling. Instantly we were swept back. An eddy caught the stern. Despite the steering oar, the stern was carried to right. Round came the bow broadside to the stream. In a moment we were end for end, and shot past a great, black, slippery stone, within six inches of it. It would have staved our boat like an egg! A moment more, and we were back in the eddy whence we started, completely winded and spent.

"Oh-h-h! Such a current!" panted Scott. "But was n't that a close shave, — that rock!"

"Touch and a go!" muttered Fred. "Made my hair stand! We should have gone out of her in a hurry if we had struck it! There in that awful current, too, — seven or eight feet deep there!"

We got breath and eased our aching muscles.

"No use to try it up the middle there again," said Farr. "But we may possibly get up between the rock and the alders, on the left side. One thing — I 'm going to try a setting-pole instead of the oars this time."

"A good idea," said Fred.

We landed a little below and cut a strong ash sapling, which Farr cut off at twelve feet or thereabouts. With this he took my place in the stern, and I took his oars.

"Now be ready to do your prettiest this time," said Fred. "Keep her going if you can. Don't let her stop and hang in the current. Let 's see if we can't go up at the first spurt, and have it done quick. Ready now. Every time I yell '*Hi!*' every man dip his oar, sharp. Now for it once more! — *Hi! hi! hi!*"

We went at the rapid again with fresh courage.

"*Hi! hi! hi!*"

Up we went. Again the boat settled into the water. Farr sent us on with long shoves with his pole.

"*Hi! hi! hi!* — Quicker!"

Up, up, yard after yard. We were almost to the crest of the rapid when the bow swerved a foot to left: this side was full of cross currents. Scott in the bow put out his whole strength to force it back. So did Fred and myself. Too late! It turned side to the stream in a twinkling, and went round, nearly pitching Farr out with his pole. Before we could dip our oars, or Farr could regain his balance sufficiently to set the pole, the current swept us among the alders which projected out over the water, — a perfect hedge-row of them. They were clogged and laden with dirt, grass, and dry leaves, lodged among them by the recent freshet. Many of the stalks and twigs were dead and dry. We went smash among these, brushing off our hats, scratching our hands and faces, and filling our eyes with dirt, and the boat with grass and leaves! The water was deep — six or eight feet — clean under the bank. We went round and round, first one end, then the other, smashing through the alders, and brought up with a thump against a fir-trunk that had fallen out into the stream. The current still pushing us sharply, the boat tipped to one side. The water slopped in. We were stranded. Somebody let fly a few rather bad words, as we went through the alders, of which I, for one, felt ashamed afterward. This swearing over a mishap is a wicked waste of breath, and a very vulgar, foolish waste, to boot. But it was aggravating, as well as perilous.

"Worsted us again!" muttered Fred, winking the dirt out of his eyes. "Only look at the grass we've shipped. Hay enough for a shake-down."

"And alder-brush enough for a camp-fire," added Scott.

Farr was bailing out the water.

"Well, what are we going to do now?" he demanded. "Here we are — beached."

"We never can get up this rapid in the world!" exclaimed Scott. as if fully convinced of it.

"I think we might do it next time," said Fred.

"Oh, we never could!" cried Scott. "It's too strong for us."

"It would be about all we could do, anyway," Farr observed. "But I believe we can *sneak up* beside these alders."

"How's that?" I said.

"Let two of us grab hold of the bushes and pull the boat along, foot by foot, while the others fend off," exclaimed Farr. "I think we can work along up in that way. If we can't do it so, we can't at all."

"We can but try that," said Fred. "We can't be much worse off."

Scott and I took each an oar, in order to hold the boat off from the brush as much as possible. Fred and Farr lay hold of the green alder twigs that hung out over the water. First one would pull, then the other; each being sure not to let go his hold till the other had got a new one. It was slow work, but tolerably sure. We gained foot after foot, and did not lose. It was not a very stylish way, but like many another not particularly stylish method, it succeeded. We got up, after a while, past the brink of the rapid, into smooth water.

In commemoration of our exploit, we called the place Alder-Grab Rapids.

Fifty rods farther on, we came out to cleared fields on both sides of the river; but a few minutes later, and on rounding a bend, we found ourselves at the foot of another rapid, so much longer and rougher than the one we had but barely conquered, that we immediately gave up the idea of going up it. There was heard, too, the roar of a heavy cataract not far above.

"That must be Escohos Falls," said Fred, stopping to listen. "We might as well land here. We can't go much farther, anyhow. We shall have to carry round it."

Accordingly we landed at a place where there was a cart-track leading down to a ford, at low water, and drew up the boat. It was time, too. The sun had set. Only its last rays shone on the bald cap of Mount Escohos, that towered to the east of us. We were tired out. Our hands were badly blistered, particularly Scott's. We felt cross.

We meant to camp on the spot. While Farr and Fred were setting up the tent, however, Scott and myself went to attack an old pine stump for fuel on the hill above, and from that point espied a house about three fourths of a mile away. It was immediately determined to go to the house and see what could be done there. We had no romantic nonsense about camping out. We much preferred a house when there was one to be reached, and set off at once, following the old cart-road. Fred took his gun.

There was a barn as well as a house, both enclosed by a fence of rails and logs; altogether a very dilapidated establishment. The house was a sprawling, one-story affair, only partially shingled. There were no curtains to the six-pane windows; and we found, as we had suspected while yet at some distance, that it was deserted, — empty, but neither " swept " nor " garnished." The yard was full of tall thistles, with down blowing about in the wind. The door, half unhinged, stood partly agape, and among the thistles, not a yard from the log door-step, a partridge began to "quit" at our approach. Fred shot it promptly.

# CHAPTER VII.

### FIREWORKS!

THE house inside was a picture of desolation. Dirt, soot, and old bricks lay about in quantities. There were two rooms on the ground floor. One of these had been plastered, but the plaster was half off it and covered the floor. There was a queer odor about the place, — the odor of that irregular combination of ingredients known as "gurry." Some ruffian had smashed the chamber stairs with an axe (we knew it was with an axe, for there lay the axe, a particularly rusty and ugly one, with blood stains on it). So we did not at once go up-chamber.

The out-look was not inviting; no more was the *in*-look. Nevertheless, we at once decided to camp in the house.

" But somebody has got to go back to the boat after *stuff*," Fred remarked.

Nobody wanted that commission. Tired as we were, it seemed a dreadful job. Each one, even Spot, looked glum.

" Must be done," Fred argued.

Everybody looked glummer. [Glummer may or may not be good English.]

" Draw lots for it, then," urged Fred.

" That's fair," Scott admitted ; generally his luck was wonderful.

Fred broke four bits off a straw of herdsgrass.

We drew.

Greatly to his disgust, Scott got the short one. He muttered evil things. At that, Fred magnanimously offered to go with him. They set off on a tired trot, charging us to kindle a fire ; for it was already dusk.

There was a fireplace, but no andirons. Farr remedied this deficit, however, by setting up loose bricks. Fred had left us two matches. We broke up three or four rails from the straggling fence with the bloody axe (I hope it was the blood of nothing nearer man than a yearling), and soon had the deserted hearth aglow. I then started for the barn, to get hay for a bed before it should grow quite dark.

The old barn-yard was also filled with thistles, only these were bull thistles instead of Canada thistles; and here I started up two more partridges. I might have shot them as well as not, for they ran a rod or more before flying.

That's always the way. If you want to see game, leave your gun at home.

Hearing the gun when Fred shot the first, these two had probably hidden here.

Somebody had cut and stored several tons of hay in the barn the previous summer. I helped myself, bringing along as much as I could get in my arms at two loads. It filled the whole back side of the room, and considered as a bed, looked tempting.

Fred and Scott came back, toiling under the weight of kettle, frying-pan, meat, meal, flour, and potatoes. Fred had also taken along our four woollen blankets.

Water was then brought from a spring and rill, where an old barrel had been set in days past. While Fred and Scott rested on the hay, Farr and myself got on meat to fry and potatoes to boil, and we were meditating a hasty pudding, when Scott cried, " Hark! what's that rumbling and roaring?"

The old house had got afire upstairs, about the ill-constructed chimney! Then there was a lively to-do!

" Fire! fire!" Farr began to roar.

We had to take the potato-kettle, with all in it, to throw water. It was blazing like mad up through the roof on the outside. Fred got a rail and climbed up by it upon the roof (the eaves were low), and we passed up to him kettleful after kettleful of water.

He put it out without much difficulty. But that was not the worst of it. On going inside again, we found that the water had run down, wellnigh extinguishing the fire in the fireplace, and filling the spider of meat with wet cinders and soot. There was a dismal puddle on the floor, and it had run under the hay, thereby spoiling our bed utterly.

However, we had faced worse disasters than this. Fred fell to work to reproduce supper. Farr and I mopped up, using the hay, which we threw out and then got a fresh supply from the barn. Scott watched the house.

These mishaps delayed us so much that it was toward eight o'clock before supper was cooked, including the hasty pudding, which we ate with sugar only; for Scott was forever preaching against eating so much *grease*. He thought it highly injurious; and perhaps it was. It had been long since our noon lunch, and we had labored so smartly that we were ravenous, and stuffed ourselves so industriously that, together with our fatigue, we nearly dropped asleep over the last potato. Scott, however, had been in jeopardy lest the damp floor should give us our death. He roused up and strenuously insisted on a good rousing fire to dry up the moisture. None of the rest of us would stir an inch to break up more rails. So he went at it himself, and built what he called a "good rousing" one, I suppose, for I was already in a drowse. And another nice fracas that cost us! Old Scratch himself was in our luck that night. We were not ten minutes asleep, when another "rumbling and roaring" began. First Fred, then all of us, jumped up, suddenly disturbed by it.

"'House's afire again!'" Fred shouted.

But it wasn't the house this time; it was the chimney. The old thing was foul as a blackguard, no doubt. Very likely it had never

IT BLEW THE OVEN-DOOR CLEAR ACROSS THE ROOM.

been burned out and was chock full of soot. Scott's rousing fire had touched it off.

How it roared! We sat aghast at it. A big freight train rumbling over a long bridge was all I could think of. Perceiving a mighty illumination outside, we ran out. There was a sight for a dark night! The place was light as day! A column of fire was going out the top of that old chimney, twenty feet high, if it was an inch! I never saw anything like that before. And the air fairly *sung* in through the old door, it drew so hard. It was dazzlingly bright, and gained strength every minute. The column even grew in height. Great red clots of soot flew up like rockets; and a shower of sparks and cinders was falling. Before we knew it, the old roof was blazing in three or four places. Farr ran for the potato-kettle, and we threw water fast and hard. We soon put out the fire in the shingles. Fred meanwhile had climbed up into the chamber by the ruins of the old stairs, and was calling to bring water at the top of his voice. It had caught all around the chamber floor, and about the roof beneath. Then we worked again. Water in the kettle, in the frying-pan, and in both of Scott's rubber boots, as fast as we could all three run with it! and Fred upstairs dousing it on the fire! The chamber floor leaked like a thunder shower, and there was a stench of soot so pungently powerful that it was like facing a pepper-mill to enter the door.

Fred put out the fire.

"But this chimney's red-hot!" he shouted down to us. "Hisses like a demon when the water touches it! Pass up another kettleful; I'll stand ready to throw."

Farr had run to put out another blaze on the outside of the roof; and Scott and I were hoisting up the kettle to Fred, when there came a report as loud as a gun from near the fireplace. It was from inside the old brick and stone oven; and it blew the oven door off its leather hinges clear across the room!

Whether there was powder or anything of that sort in the oven left there, or whether it was gas from the soot that exploded, we could not find out.    Fred came down the staircase at a jump.

" If this old shebang is going to blow up," said he, " I 'll be getting down.    I believe it 's haunted, or bewitched !"

The oven was aglow with soot-coal that had tumbled down the flue ; but we could detect nothing else ; and yet we had hardly turned away before there came a second explosion, that blew the glowing coal out the mouth and all over the room.    We did not know what to make of that ; never have known.    Scientific students, perhaps, can account for it.

This thing disturbed us worse than all the rest.    We kept well out of the range of the oven-mouth after that.

It went off once or twice afterwards, but not so loud.

Gradually the pillar of fire from the chimney went down ; though it burned an hour or over in all.    If anybody saw it at a distance, it must have been an astonishing spectacle.    Once or twice while we were carrying water, I heard the surprised cries of wild animals from the side of Escohos.    Poor Spot had retreated out to the water-barrel, where he greeted us each time we came out with imploring wags of his tail ; and once, when the thistles in the yard had caught fire, he howled dolorously.

The flames subsided, but for a long while the inside of the chimney remained in a bright red coal.    It shone up into the air ; and the great draught continued to set up the flue.    It had got so hot that we did not dare to leave it, and so sat up and watched it.

Finally Fred climbed up from the outside and threw a frying-pan of water into it, at the top.    This raised a prodigious hissing ; and a vast volume of steam flew up.    But a few frying-panfuls sensibly cooled it, or, at least, blackened it ; for the fierce glow died out.    Darkness gathered in.

The fireplace was drenched with water, the hay soaked ten times worse than before; and the chamber floor dripped like a subterranean cavern. The house was quite uninhabitable.

" Let's go to the barn," said Farr; " and try that."

" It 's long past midnight," Scott declared.

We brushed through the bull-thistles, shoved the lean-to door open, and felt our way to the mow. Into this we crept, and burying ourselves in the hay, soon dropped asleep.

Altogether that was an exhausting day.

# CHAPTER VIII.

## A HARD CARRY.

WHEN I unglued my eyes next morning, it was broad daylight out of doors. Farr was sitting up on end, very busily engaged. I had to look twice before I fully comprehended the extent and design of his labors, — and so would you, reader.

He was keel-hauling his pants. He had ravelled out about four inches of the leg of one of his knit stockings, and was darning the seat of his pants with the yarn. There was ingenuity and resource!

Seeing me awake and attentive, he grinned sardonically.

"What's the use of *legs* to stockings," said he, with a fine scorn in his tone, "unless you use them for repairs? They do no good. Always getting wet, and then staying wet around your shanks."

"But they're handy things to have about one," he added, after a pause filled with long stitches.

"Wherever did you get that darn-needle?" I inquired.

"Oh, that's the one I've always had," replied the repairer. "That's another handy thing to have, — a darn-needle; good for splinters, good for mending, good for picking out the tube of your gun, good for a hundred things. I would n't travel without one. Why, a darn-needle 's a thing you can fall back on 'most any time."

Ah, it was grim business to stir and get up that morning. We were sore, lame, stiff, and felt old all over: we had over-exerted ourselves. Too much exercise is not quite so bad as none at all, however; it leaves one tougher for next time.

Scott got up cross, and grumbled at everything, till Farr sung out to him, " Look o' here, you man that fired the chimney, shut up ! "

Fred, too, was rather quiet that morning, but busied himself getting breakfast. We built a fire out in the yard; we had had enough of the house. Our wet blankets we hung on the fence to dry in the brisk morning breeze.

Fred made another batch of " flippers ; " and those, with coffee, brightened us up a good deal.

Leaving our kitchen property at the house, we all four set off in the direction of the falls to "prospect" for a team to draw our boat across the carry. There was what the Magallowayans call a road ; though it might have found difficulty in passing as such almost anywhere else. We followed it confidently. Wilson's Mills were somewhere ahead.

The path crooked about among spruce and fir thickets. Quite suddenly we met a dog, — a monster ; so big that we all involuntarily shied from him. He was brindled and had a mighty pink muzzle and fine surly eyes, out of which he merely threw us a passing glance. Spot cut out into the bushes and made a great circle around him.

" Heavens ! what a dog !" Scott exclaimed, glancing civilly back after him. " The biggest dog I ever saw in all my life !"

" Brought up on bear's meat," Farr suggested.

Another turn brought us out in sight of two red houses, three barns, and a schoolhouse, the latter so small that at first we took it for a corn-crib. We made for the first red house, and a very comfortable sort of house it was, for the region. A bright-looking little fellow stood in the door-way ; but before we had got quite near enough to accost him, three more dogs rushed out, each larger than the other; though none of them quite equalled the one we had met. Catching sight of Spot, they made for him, barking and growling like furies. Spot wedged himself betwixt Farr's legs, and having no farther retreat, growled defiance. Fred clubbed his long shot-gun, and whirling it around in a lively manner, knocked the smallest one over, and put the others to flight.

The little boy looked on dispassionately. I was glad to see that he appeared to regard it as a proper thing to do.

Said Scott, " What 's your name, my boy? "

" I 'm not your boy," said the child.   " I 'm papa's boy."

" Right.   What is your papa's name? "

" His name is Spoff."

" Yes, — and is Mr. Spoff at home? "

Something about this prefix of *Mr.* seemed to strike the boy as not being just right, but he got over it and told us that " Spoff " was gone up the Diamond.

At this juncture a young woman came to the door.   A glance indicated that it was the boy's mother.   Scott raised his cap.

" Good-morning, Mrs. Spoff," said he.   " The little boy tells me that Mr. Spoff is not at home."

A little to our surprise, the lady first smiled, then laughed merrily.

" Did Frankie tell them papa's name was Spoff? " looking with arch reproof into the little fellow's upturned face, while she playfully rumpled his hair.

Then she explained to us, — " My husband's name is Flint, — Spofford Flint.   But persons sometimes call him Spoff, for short. That 's what Frankie has got hold of."

Scott begged pardon.

" Why, it was Frankie's mistake," she said.

A very pretty woman was Mrs. Flint.   Finer eyes I have rarely seen.   Her air and manners were those of a lady.   She was frank and agreeable.   We supposed, at the time, that she had not always resided on the Magalloway; but I have since learned that we were wrong in our surmise.   Well, Nature can make a lady as well as good society, and now and then does.

Scott explained that we were wishing to pass the falls, and had hoped to be able to make a bargain with Mr. Flint to draw our boat over the carry.

"I can have it done for you," said she, promptly. "Do you wish to go over immediately?"

We did.

"Very well; walk in, please, and wait a few moments, till I can send our man."

But we thought it better to return at once to the boat, to get it out of the river and pack up our luggage. This we did, and had hardly done so, when the man, "Pete" (whom we had heard Mrs. Flint call), made his appearance, leading a strong black mare harnessed to a long cart. Pete was a French Canadian of the prevailing pattern; and the black mare was a veritable Tartar, bearing the pretty name of Jenny.

'T was a round load for her: that heavy boat with all our traps and bags. All the time we were loading and lashing the boat fast with many turns of the rope, Jenny kept turning the white of a vicious eye round to us. She highly disapproved of the whole proceedings. On getting the word to go, the gentle brute instantly let fly her heels high over the load, and went the wrong way, to wit, backwards, and came near depositing the cart in the rapids, at the outset.

But Pete was not wholly unprepared. He clubbed the white-oak whip-stock, and laid the heavy end across the recalcitrant Jenny. "*Herret, Jennáy! herret!*" he screamed.

He knew only three or four English words; but had fully mastered our great national oath. This he bestowed on "Jennáy" without stint.

"Is n't it strange that that is the first thing these fellows learn of our talk?" Fred said to me as we followed after the cart. "Never saw one so green yet but that he knew so much English."

Mrs. Flint was in the yard as we came along the road past the house. We stopped to pay for the job of drawing the boat.

" Three dollars," she said, was what they had for taking a boat over the carry.

With " Spoff " himself we might have chaffered for less, — not with her. Fred and I paid it, with cheerful alacrity, between us ; though it reduced our united capital to two dollars and twenty-five cents.

A little beyond the Flints, the carry path diverges from the road, and leads up through a pasture for a hundred rods or more, then enters the woods. This pasture is the extreme limit of the cleared land on the river. Beyond it lay the great wilderness. At this place the Magalloway falls over a long succession of ledges down the ravine between Escohos and " Parker Hill," so called. I do not know that the entire height of the fall has ever been calculated. For a guess, I should place it at from two hundred to two hundred and fifty feet.

It is a great place for trout-fishing.

The carry is two and a half miles in length. As you go up through the pasture from Flint's there is a good view of the river valley below, and of a great semi-circular black mountain to the west of it, called the " Half-moon." From the top of Escohos, there is said to be one of the best views to be had from any mountain in New England. Some tourists think it superior to that from Mount Washington.

But we had no time to climb mountains for fine views. Our business was of a much more practical character. It was not, however, without some regrets and secret misgivings that we turned for a last look at the houses in the valley below us, then entered the woods. From this point to the head of Parmachenee it is forty-six miles. The vast wilderness before us was not without its charm, nor yet its aspect of peril and mystery.

Feelings of this sort were straightway banished by the more exciting details of the way. On entering the forest, the trail at once changed from a dry, though rough, cart-road to an exceedingly wet and muddy one. Sloughs of muck began to disclose themselves. Roaring

JENNY LEAPED AND PLUNGED LIKE A WOOD-DEMON.

brooks which dashed across the path had dug it asunder in the midst, leaving great stones plump in the way. About, among, athwart, and over these "Jennáy" leaped and plunged like a wood-demon. Everything not lashed in the strongest manner was speedily shaken off. At intervals of six or eight rods we would have to re-bestow the load. That the cart held together was a growing wonder!

Pete drove — when he could keep up. Farr and Scott ran on the off side, to hold the load on. Fred and I sought to do the same thing on the other side. Sometimes we did it, sometimes we did not. The mare went by starts and jerks; and there was no knowing when she meant to start, or when she meant to stop, after starting. She had, moreover, a most peculiar and effective way of hurling the mud from her hoofs. It was impossible to dodge it; so we hung to the load and took what came to us. But there was *spitting!* I recollect that one lump, large as one's two fists and soft as pig's grease, took Scott plump on the mouth. He let go, sputtered, and fairly gagged.

At length we came to a slough so soft and long that Pete stopped.

"No passé," he said. "Hattie" (Mrs. Flint) "not know dees!"

Scott and Farr argued, urged, and raged at him. Pete would not start the horse. It did no good to tell him we had paid to be carried across. He did not, or else would not, understand it.

"Let's take the reins away from him and drive through ourselves," Farr said.

But that seemed a rather summary way of behaving. Besides, if we should get Jenny irretrievably mired, the responsibility would lie with us. Fred quietly drew Pete aside and took out his wallet. First he showed him twenty-five cents. Pete brightened a little, but shook his head. Fred judiciously hesitated awhile, then took out a fifty cent bill. Pete was shrewd; having seen that Fred had a fifty and a twenty-five cent scrip, he at once set his price.

"Seventy-five cent!" he said, and stuck for that.

Farr was for pitching him into the slough without further ado.

Scott thought we had best go back to get authority from Mrs. Flint. But the distance was nearly two miles; and the road was fearful. We shrank, too, from involving her in the fuss, though it was clearly one in which she was interested.

On the whole, we concluded to give Pete his "seventy-five cent;" but Farr declared that he would thrash him as soon as we came out to the river. Peter was more or less of a swindler. On getting the money, however, he at once started Jenny into the slough. And in the tussle that followed, we nearly forgave the Frenchman: that was a slough such as John Bunyan might have parabled. If Jenny had not been a most remarkable animal, we should have stuck there for good.

Once out of this slough, however, the way improved. We had reached the height of land, and now turned down the heavily wooded slope toward the river. But we had lost a linchpin from the hind axle; and while in full career the wheel rolled off! It was put on again; but the wooden pins we substituted kept breaking.

"Watch!" Pete admonished, pointing to it. "Watch!"

Fred watched, with fresh pins ready.

The upper end of the falls, where we came out of the carry-road a few minutes later, is a very wild-looking place.

The stream, black as ink and overhung with straggling spruce, rolls tumultuously down over huge stones. The roar is heavy and continuous. Some of the "pitches" show a perpendicular fall of twenty feet or more. In one of these a lumberman had been drowned the previous spring. His name — "Jack Abram" — is cut in a spruce trunk at the foot of the pitch.

Above this point there is smooth water up to "The Narrows," ten miles.

The boat was taken off the cart and launched, and the luggage stowed as before. Jenny's head was then turned homeward. She was covered with mud, a complete crust of it. Scant as was our stock of potatoes, Fred gave her a couple. Used to nothing but abuse from Pete, the mare was manifestly astonished. She looked at Fred in a singular way, but took the potatoes.

Pete came to shake hands with us at parting.

" Good-by," I said to him.

" Goo'-by," said he.

But Farr would not shake hands with him.

" He's a skunk, any way," quoth our comrade; but he did not put his threat of thrashing him into execution.

For my own part, I fancy that both Pete and Jenny well earned all the money they got from us; though Pete's ruse to raise the price was a little irregular.

# CHAPTER IX.

## NIGHT IN THE WOODS.

IT was half-past two, afternoon. We had eaten nothing since breakfast. On the carry we had felt hungry; but now that noon was past we were less so, and decided to go on for a couple of hours, then camp for the night. So much for a well-established habit of taking our dinner at noon.

Above the falls the river averages from six to ten rods in width. It is deep and black, — an aspect enhanced by the fir forest on either bank, dark-green, sombre, and profoundly quiet. There were few birds here at this season, or, as I am inclined to believe, at any season. The most noticeable feature about the stream is its silence. The current creeps on steadily. If you stop rowing, it drags you slowly back; and you would not know that you were drifting unless your eye caught sight of a twig, or a bit of bough, coming slowly to meet you. The crooks and bends are numerous; but the forest is so dense here that one cannot see just how much he is the sport of them; and that is one comfort.

As we paddled on, following all these meanderings, the impression grew that we might get so involved that to get out would be impossible. In an hour we had faced every point of the compass. The general course of the stream is from north to south; but a stranger could never have guessed it, that first afternoon above the falls. The peaks of moderately high mountains on both sides of the river valley were from time to time to be seen over the fir tops. Escohos was alternately behind and fronting us; then to left or right. A tall, dark hill known as " Emery's Misery " played similar tricks. We conjectured at random as to the origin of this odd name. Beaver Hill, a pine-clad ridge to the east of the valley, was more easily accounted for.

Above Escohos we saw but few ducks, and those at a distance. Not a duck was shot till we arrived on the lake. Occasionally a great blue heron (*Ardea Herodias*) would start up, breaking the silence with its heavy flappings. Several times we shot after them in the air, but never brought down anything.

At rather unfrequent intervals, a kingfisher would spring his rattle, and go noisily up the stream in advance of us. But Fred assured us that they were not nearly so plentiful here as on the upper course of the Androscoggin.

Here and there a sluggish brook made in through the bank, showing a slim channel fringed with melancholy alders. Another shrub, however, began to attract our attention, and from henceforth made one of the most agreeable features of the river scenery. Cling-ing to the bank and leaning out over the water, we now began to note the vivid red clusters of mountain ash, or round-wood, berries. With every mile they grew more and more plentiful, till sometimes both banks presented a bright scarlet border, often reflected in the still dark water with wonderful fidelity.

Here for the first time we saw a Canada jay, sitting observant of our progress on a fir stub. It is a bird not common in southern Maine; not so handsome as its congener, the noisy blue jay, though of about the same size. Its note is even less agreeable, which is saying little enough for it as a musician. Its colors are brown and white. The lumbermen call it the carrion bird, and have also bestowed upon it two other names, even less ornate.

Scott shot at the first one we saw, with the rifle from the boat. The slug struck into the stub directly under where it had perched, and this, together with the report, set it a-scolding at a great rate. It rose a yard perhaps from where it had sat, but immediately resumed its place. The bird is not nearly as shy as the blue jay.

It was already past four o'clock. We were bethinking ourselves of stopping to camp, when Fred called our attention to what seemed an opening a little back from the river on the east bank. We drew in ashore; and Farr mounted the bank, which was higher than usual, to reconnoitre.

"Yes; there's a clearing," he called down to us. "It's where they've been cutting out spruce. And there's a shanty."

"What say, — shall we go out to it?" Fred queried.

I was afraid that it might be lousy; but the others did not agree with me. We tied the boat to a fir trunk, and took out our ducks and the partridge, which we supposed had been kept about as long as they should be, together with our guns, the inevitable and never-to-be-left-behind potato kettle, frying-pan, etc. (These utensils are always understood to be present unless forgotten.)

The shanty was on rising ground about a hundred rods from the stream. It was built of spruce logs with a shed roof of pine " splits," — the usual shanty of the backwoods, — with a "split" door secured by a wooden pin. Farr was ahead, and had the first peep.

"Here's luck!" he sang out to us.

There was a cooking-stove all set up, just as the last logging gang had left it. Possibly they intended to use the shanty during the coming winter; for there was a barrel half full of salt pork in the brine, and a barrel containing beans, also a small quantity of tea in an old salt-box. And what we liked better still, they had nearly half a cord of wood cut stove-length. It was tiered up at one end of the shanty, and was dry as tinder.

To get supper with such accommodations seemed nothing but fun.

In another barrel Fred speedily unearthed a whole set of tin plates, cups, basins, and baker-sheets.

Half an hour later we had a duck and a partridge parboiling, potatoes cooking, and a batch of Horsford biscuit baking. The old stove, with its front doors and top red-hot, had a most home-like aspect: we felt quite happy.

That was one of the most enjoyable suppers on the river. I say on the river, since it could not, of course, compare with some of those sumptuous barbecues after we got fairly established at the head of the lake. No meals that I ever ate could indeed compare with those. For then we had grand living and grand appetites together.

It had never seemed like really camping in the wilderness, till that night. Before, when we had camped at Moll's Rock, we knew that there was a settlement not ten miles above us; but here we knew we were fairly launched in the forest, — a forest that extended even into Canada and to the Gulf of St. Lawrence. The woods, too, had a different *seeming*. A wilder quiet rested over all, broken now and then by wilder sounds.

While we were eating, a bear cried out from the hill-side back of the shanty: a plaintive cry, like that of some forlorn and benighted maiden wandering in the darkening forest. Neither Scott nor myself would have known what it was, but for the ready interpretation of Fred's practised ear.

"I would not wonder if we might get a shot at him, by all starting out with our guns and getting around him," said he; "as soon as he heard any one of us he would run, and make such a noise in the brush that some of us might get a shot."

We were all tired, however; and, to tell the truth, did not much relish the idea of such a hunt in the night. Besides, there was some danger of shooting each other by mistake.

As the evening advanced other cries, generally at a considerable distance, broke the stillness. Various prowlers were abroad. A sharp, raspy screech resounded on a sudden, seemingly from near where we had tied up the boat. It made us start sharply, it was so near and ugly. The next moment it was followed by a deep *tu-whit-tu-whooo-oo!*

"Nothing but a screech-owl," said Fred.

These dense fir and spruce forests on the river seemed a populous haunt of owls.

There was a long bunk, bedded with boughs, on the back side of the shanty. We closed and pinned the door; then rolling up in our blankets, lay down and talked till we fell asleep.

But along in the night we were awakened by a great racket on the roof of dry splits over our heads. Something was digging, scratching, and tearing them up. They rattled prodigiously. We all jumped up into sitting posture.

"What on earth is that?" demanded Scott, in an alarmed whisper.

"I don't know," said Fred.

"Means to dig down to us!" Farr said. "Smells us!"

"Thinks there's something *hurting* down here," said Fred.

"I'll fix him!" Scott whispered. "Keep quiet."

We got out of the bunk and fumbled out one of the guns, — Farr's double-barrelled one. We heard him cocking it.

"Don't hold the muzzle too near the splits," Fred cautioned.

But he did hold it too near, and fired both barrels at once. It made a stunning report, and recoiled violently out of his hands. So great was the pressure that the splits were blown up off the poles, for they were not nailed down.

Almost at the same instant I heard something leap off on to the ground. Fred opened the door and shouted *st — boy!* to Spot. Out bounded Spot, barking furiously; but he didn't run far. Before we had even time to step out, he came back with a yelp and scooted into the door, betwixt our legs!

Farr struck a match and lighted some dry splints. The blaze disclosed Spot glaring out at the door, the hair on his back raised and stiff as bristles, and his tail straight as a cob.

SPOT GLARING OUT AT THE DOOR.

Fred began to laugh. " You 'll get eaten up, Spot, as sure as fate," said he.

We went out and listened. It was too dark to see much ; and the cleared space was full of old spruce tops and low shrubs. We heard once what seemed the stealthy snap of a twig. Farr let fly a slug from the rifle. The light of the discharge lit up the brush ; but we saw nothing and heard nothing more.

" Lucivee, I guess," said Fred. " Smelled our cookery, and so jumped up on the splits to sharpen his claws."

It took some little time to get quieted down enough to go to sleep, after this rouse-up ; but we had a good morning nap.

# CHAPTER X.

## GLOWING PLANS.

IT was after sunrise before we were astir, and nearly eight before we started for the boat.

We left the old shanty as good as we found it, save for the blackening of the splits and several buck-shot holes through them, where Scott had fired at our nocturnal disturber. We took along enough buttered Horsfords (biscuits, the reader must understand) to serve for our noon lunch, so as not to have to delay to kindle a fire and cook.

The morning was beautiful, cloudless and mild, with a lingering breath of summer in the breeze. The sun shone warmly, yet softly. We were in uncommon spirits, and sang and whistled for pure love of the thing. Times came when we had to do it to keep up our spirits; but none of those things troubled us that morning. We made the old bateau shoot through the water, and laughed at the puniness of the current. But currents are things that hold their own better than exuberant spirits.

We had rowed perhaps two miles, when a low roar of rushing waters began to be heard. It grew more distinct, till rounding a bend, we saw where the stream pours forcefully between two ledges, not more than forty feet apart.

"The Narrows," said Fred. "Now for something like work."

At the foot of the cascade there is a great eddy, flanked by reaches of dead water. We pulled up into the eddy within a hundred feet of the bottom of the rapid, then stopped to take a look and deliberate.

The ledges mark the difference of level between the lower and the upper portions of the river valley. The length of the rapid is not over twenty yards, at most, and the descent not more than four or five feet. Yet the current was wonderfully swift, and sucked through the narrow passage with a strength that we had not quite expected.

"Can we run it?" said Farr, doubtfully.

"Well, we can try," Fred replied. "We're fresh this morning. It's a mere question of muscle. There are no rocks in the way, and it isn't a long pull."

"All right," Scott exclaimed. "Draw wind for it!"

As usual, I had the stern seat and steering-paddle.

"Head her right straight into it," Fred advised. "Don't let her swerve a hair. Punch her nose right through it! All ready now. *One* — ONE — ONE!"

We struck, every one together and with full strength on. The bateau went into it like a steam ram. We could feel her head going up.

"She's mounting!" Fred shouted. "At it!"

*Plash — plash!* dipped the oars.

The downward current gurgled loudly against us and put out all its mighty strength to drive us back. We struck hard and fast to conquer it, and gained, though more and more slowly, till we got into the narrowest place. There we stuck as in a vice.

A minute of utmost exertion, — then back we went, turned in the eddy, and lodged in the dead water under the right bank.

Then there was panting and puffing, and cooling of burning palms in the water. I had raised a blister in less than two minutes!

"Gracious! isn't that a strong draft!" Scott exclaimed.

"A regular suck-hole," said Farr.

"What think of it now, Fred?" I queried.

"It seems as if we ought to do it," said Fred; "the place is so short, we ought to get up it."

" Yes, it 's short — but, oh, Moses! " laughed Farr. " There 's one way, and only one way: that is, to get up full speed before we strike into the sluice-way there. We must back her down below the eddy, then start and get the boat under full headway. If we do that, and pull like *all possessed*, we may go up."

This seemed reasonable.

We rested some minutes and got breath, then dropped down with the current fifty or sixty yards.

" We 'll drive her up this time," Farr said confidently.

But first we shifted the load somewhat, in order to bring the nose higher in the water.

" Are you all ready ? " Fred demanded of us.

" All ready."

" Well, then, — *hi ! hi ! hi !* "

We dashed through the eddy at full jump, went into the rapid again, and climbed up, up, up, almost to where the smooth black stream bent downward. Every muscle now!

" Wake up! " yelled Fred; " wake up! One yard more! One more! "

We should have done it, I am sure we should. We *were doing it*, when I let the nose swerve a foot, — no more. I could n't help it. It was done quick as a wink. Another moment, and we were overmatched and swept back into the eddy, and into the self-same place under the right bank.

" That was almost, but not quite," exclaimed Fred, dubiously.

" If you had only kept her head straight," lamented Scott.

Yes; I knew that as well as anybody. Such a blunder cuts a fellow awfully. Neither Fred nor Farr found a word of fault; but the thing spoke for itself.

" What say to trying the line ? " Farr proposed. " We don't want to lay on too many blisters at one heat."

We had a sixty-foot line, taken along for such emergencies. It was got out. We then pulled up to the foot of the rapid on the left bank, and landed Farr and Scott. One end of the line was now knotted into the ring in the bow, and the other end thrown to them. They climbed round the base of the ledges, and straightening the rope, began to draw on it. It was a rather ticklish business. Fred and I had our hands full to fend off with our oars, and hold the boat from being dashed against the jagged sides. But "slow and steady" did it.

Once in the smooth water above the rapid, we recoiled our line and went on, — a little chagrined, however, at having had to use it. When a fellow sets out to go by water, he naturally wants to do so.

It was ten o'clock. We thought the current a little swifter above the Narrows than below; not much. The fir forest continued; but there were higher banks, with occasional rocks. The profusion of round-woods increased rather than diminished.

A little past twelve we stopped at a pole camp, on a low bluff, to eat our Horsfords and drain off what coffee there remained over in the coffee-pot from breakfast.

This camp is known as "Lincoln Pond Brook Camp." The brook that here makes in is the outlet of Lincoln Pond, lying off to the east of the river.

A tree near by proclaimed this to be "a —— starvation country." But we had not found it so, thus far. Not only do many of the firs along this river have a sylvan language of their own, but they seem to have adopted the language of men, — and a very profane and ribald tongue we found it. It at least shows what sort of company they have kept. Trees that talk like those have no business in good society. And lest they should corrupt the morals of some innocent and untutored tourist, we took the liberty of "spotting" off some of their unblushing ribaldry with the axe. This we did the more sedulously since we had heard that an adventurous party of young ladies from New York were intending to penetrate this region the next summer.

That they should fall in with such scurrilous trees was not to be thought of; and we could think of no better way to reform them.

We gave ourselves twenty minutes for dinner.

Not long after, we passed Metallic Pond, — a pretty little expanse opening into the Magalloway by a broad outlet on the west side. There are two Metallic Ponds. The other is on the east side of the river, and is not in sight from it.

An hour later we emerged from the evergreen forest, and saw, stretching off to the north of us, a great tract of open land set here and there with large elms.

" The meadows," said Fred.

We had reached the foot of those famous natural meadows of the Magalloway, which extend for twelve miles along the banks, and are of themselves well worth a visit. Originally, I presume, there may have been a lake here, the bed of which the forest has not yet encroached upon. Some enterprising farmer, with a few thousand dollars' capital, might put this whole tract into good grass and make a fortune in hay. For hay in this region often sells for thirty dollars per ton at the logging camps.

Cranberries, too, might be cultivated on many hundred acres of this meadow, with profit, no doubt.

We talked of all these chances of gain, as we rowed on.

" If we cannot make money any other way, we will just come up here and settle," Fred would say, after each argument of the chances.

We grew quite enthusiastic over the beauty and extent of this great alluvial bottom; and I still think it would have been a nice opening for us four boys, if we had obtained a permit and settled there. I am quite sure that for every dollar we now have, we might have had five, if we had had the perseverance to carry out the plans we laid there that pleasant October afternoon.

I am the more confident of this, that I have since known four young fellows from the city, who left town and took up a similar plantation in the wilderness. Their adventures and experiences (of which one of their number has kindly furnished me some account) were so amusing, pleasant, and sometimes so exciting, that I have often regretted not being one of their party. I doubt whether four youngsters ever had a better time than they had, and are still having. Add to these pleasures of pioneer life the robust health they have ever enjoyed, and the reader will agree with me that they are really to be envied by the whole army of pale clerks on their high stools, who still cling to the city and its pitiful salaries. White hands and stylish coats are good things enough in their way, no doubt, but not to be set against vigor, fresh air, liberty, and plenty of cash, in my humble opinion.

My four friends above alluded to have now a backwoods farm, or rather plantation, worth fifty thousand dollars, which yields them a net profit of from twelve to fifteen thousand a year. They come as near being kings as we tolerate here in America. Nothing would tempt them to go back to clerking. And when I consider how much unoccupied territory we have, even in the State of Maine, that might be taken up in the same way, and how full the cities are of poorly paid young men, I really wish that more would do as these four have done. They would be happier, healthier, and make more money; and the country at large would be the better for it. But everybody must follow his own *bent*, I suppose, if he has one.

Even here the round-woods continued to fringe the banks and hang out their profusion of red berries. There were great quantities, too, of high-bush cranberries.

The current is swifter through the meadows than we had generally found it below. It perceptibly increased the labor of rowing, and at some points was about as much as we could comfortably breast. Through the meadows, too, the stream was seemingly more crooked than below; the crooks were not so broad, but sharper and more of them. Contrary to what would be expected here, the bed of the stream is sandy in many places, often disclosing sandy spits and beaches. At one of these latter there was a board stuck up in the sand, on which was chalked in red, —

"This is Turkle Government."

But we saw no turkles (turtles) here, though somebody has, no doubt. I think that it was nine herons Scott saw along the meadows, and kept the account of.

But a more interesting ornithological fact came out in connection with this locality. Soon after entering on the meadows we began to hear the "kiff" of robins, and saw scores of these birds all about on the elms. It seemed a robins' paradise. As we went on, the air fairly resounded to their sharp notes. They were feasting on the great banquet of round-wood berries which Nature has here set out for them, — a banquet that to exhaust would be impossible. There were hundreds — I may safely say thousands — of robins about the meadows; and it was their presence that gave the locality so great a charm for us.

And now I have a fact for naturalists, — one I hope they will receive as given on good authority. When we came back down the river on the ice, seven weeks later (about the first of December), we still saw robins here, though not in so great numbers. There was then nearly a foot of snow. The weather was cold, and had been very cold indeed. In a word, it was severe winter weather. The round-woods were still red with the frozen fruit; and the robins were contentedly *billing* it off.

Two lumbermen at Errol, New Hampshire, told me that on one occasion they had seen robins here in February, and on another, in January. He confidently asserted that many robins winter here, whenever it is a good season for round-wood berries. This fact acquires some importance, when it is remembered that these "meadows" are in about the latitude of Montreal. I know of no other instance or locality where the robin has been known to pass the winter so far north.

As we drew near the head of the meadows, we saw numerous

I FELLED A WHITE BIRCH.

bluffs covered with fir and spruce, and occasionally with pine. These were, no doubt, islands of the old-time lake. It was getting near sunset, and we resolved to camp on one of these, past the very foot of which the river ran. It rose fifteen or twenty feet above the surrounding bottom, and was wooded with a mixed growth of white birch, fir, spruce, and hornbeam.

The boat was hitched to a stout sapling of this latter wood; and while Fred and Scott set up the A tent, Farr and I felled a white birch and slivered an old pine stump. From the bark of the former and the fat splinters of the latter, a cheerful blaze was soon crackling.

The reader can easily guess of what our supper consisted. So I have no need to print the bill of fare, though it was by no means a long one.

Fred took a dipper, however, while Farr was frying meat, and going down the bank, gathered a dessert to make our meal relish better, — a dessert of high-bush cranberries. I liked the taste of these pretty well. Scott detested them. Thus do tastes differ.

After supper we cut more wood, built a glorious fire, then sprigged a grand bed of the boughs. On this, with the flap of the tent buttoned back, we lay enjoying an after-supper hour of rest. But this is a luxury that only a tired voyager can fully appreciate.

There was a glorious yellow twilight, glowing over the black evergreen ridges and peaks to the west of the valley. We watched it die off, and not very long after died off ourselves — in profound slumber. There were no disturbing " lucivees " that night. If owls saluted our fire, we heard them not. Whatever savage eyes glowered at us in our white tent, we recked not of them. We were, to use Farr's ornate phrase, " putting the slumber into ourselves; " slumber being an article that must be taken in like water and food.

# CHAPTER XI.

### SHOALS AND SHALLOWS.

FRED kindly got up and built a fire that morning before waking the rest of us; and this was only one of his fatherly ways.

It seemed like a late April morning. There was that in the air that reminded us of spring: the same light, gauzy mists were rising from the ground; and out on the elms the robins sang, as in nest-making time. The illusion was almost perfect. Only the red cranberry clusters and the bunches of round-wood plums marred the fancy.

We breakfasted immediately and went on. The stream had fallen several inches during the night. The high water from the freshet was subsiding.

Two miles more of meadow, and we had again entered the fir woods, leaving the meadow with its robins behind.

"Now bowse ahead, fellows!" Fred exhorted. "On to Parmachenee! We ought to reach the foot of the lake to-night."

"Bowse ahead," I may remark, had been our motto all the way up. It is not, I am aware, a very elegant one; but in tight places we had found it expressive, — more forcible than mere "go ahead."

And we had need *to bowse;* for immediately after leaving the meadows we found ourselves in a very long and tiresome rapid, though not a very violent one. Before we reached the comparatively moderate water above, we had taken the morning kinks well out of our muscles.

A mile above are the "Great Rips."

These we reached twenty minutes later. The banks on both sides are here very unfavorable for using the tow-line; and to get up without it was quite out of the question.

"We shall have to take to the water," Fred declared, at a glance.

The "rip," or rapid, is a hundred yards in length; and the water runs pretty roughly, with a clearly defined roar; all these descents have each a distinct and peculiar voice; some harsh, gruff, and ominous, others mellow, and still others cheery, though brawling.

"How deep is the water?" Scott queried; "and will it not take a fellow off his feet?"

"Pull up to the foot of it," Fred said; "and we will soon find out. It does n't look deep."

He jumped out. It was about to his middle.

"I'll hold the boat," said he, taking hold of the nose. "Fix the line, Farr."

Farr knotted one end of the tow-line into the ring.

"Now, then, pile out," said Fred. "We'll Indian-file it up the centre."

This was our first experience of wading. Below, the stream had been far too deep. Scott hesitated a little about stepping overboard, till seeing the rest of us laughing at him, he leaped out promptly.

Nothing like a little — not too much — ridicule, to bring a fellow out.

Fred went ahead and picked the way. Farr followed next. Scott and I brought up the rear. It did not draw very hard.

We walked steadily up. The water did not, even in the holes, come above our waists. It was considerably strong. It took Scott off his feet once; but he supported himself by the rope. We were not more than ten minutes getting up. After the first chill, the water did not feel cold at all. On the whole, I rather enjoyed it. Of course it left us with wet pants, etc.; but these are things one does not mind off in the woods, if the weather be not cold.

A hundred rods above this place are the Forks, with the Little Magalloway, which joins the main stream from the northwest. The Little Magalloway is not more than one third the size of the main river. It is a very pretty stream, running over bright yellow sand and pebbles. A boat can be run up for a number of miles. We had been told that a boat could be towed up the Magalloway proper as far as "The Great Eddy," one mile above the Forks; but the rips looked so formidable and continuous, that we concluded to land here and take to the carry-path. Accordingly, we pulled into the Little Magalloway, and after proceeding from sixty to eighty rods, for a guess, landed at the place where many former voyagers seemed to have moored their boats, and where, indeed, Godwin had advised us to land at the outset.

Here were the traces of numerous camp-fires. Trees had been felled for fuel. As it was near noon, we determined to have dinner before attempting to cross the carry. From this point to the foot of the lake it is four miles, so called. It cannot be less. My own impression is that it is five, certainly. It seemed ten before we got our bateau across it next day.

Above "The Great Eddy" there are continuous falls, clean up to the dam at the lake. There is a fairly defined carry-path through the woods, though trees have fallen across it in many places. This path was "bushed out" some years previously by the lumbermen when the Berlin Mills Company logged on the lake, and built the dam at the foot of it.

Here, as at other places, the trees had a good deal to say. One large spruce declared, —

"This is a fine wild country, but lacks good grub and ladies' society."

Another fir put a query respecting the origin of the name *Magalloway*. It asked, —

"Is Magalloway an Indian name, or simply from *My-gall's-away?*"

IMMEDIATELY WE BEGAN TO FIND TREES ACROSS THE PATH BREAST-HIGH.

Still another profane hemlock swore fearfully about the length of the carry, and the tree-trunks across it. Scott indignantly rebuked it — with the axe.

As soon as dinner was got and eaten, we drew up the bateau out of the stream, in order that it might get dry for to-morrow's task of carrying it up to the lake. Our traps, bags, etc., we then carried to a little distance and hid in a thicket of firs. We did not deem it probable that any one would pass, yet there might somebody come along; and from the profanity of the trees we gained a poor opinion of the morals of the place generally.

Our blankets, kettles, tin-ware, and raw provisions for several days were then packed up, — each pack weighing from twenty-five to thirty-five pounds. Of these, we gave Scott the lightest one. Each adjusted his pack to suit his own back. We took also our guns in our hands, and the ammunition in our pockets.

By the time we were ready to set off, it was two o'clock or after.

The path, which could only be followed by close attention, wound in and out among a heavy spruce growth, with an occasional lofty pine.

"There's a hundred dollars — in that tree," Fred would remark, pointing to one of these forest monarchs, where it towered high over the surrounding growth.

Often these pines were five or six feet in diameter, showing a clean trunk for sixty or seventy feet.

Immediately we began to find trees, spruce and fir, across the path, just as they had fallen, lying at breast height. Over the first of these we climbed without noticing the inconvenience; but after getting over a dozen or more it began to grow a very wearying business. If any reader wishes a practical idea of it, let him take a weight of thirty pounds on his shoulders, and a gun in his hand, and climb over a gate twenty or thirty times. It takes a very fair allowance of time to go a mile under such circumstances.

It was three o'clock when we reached the point where the path from "The Great Eddy" joins the main carry-path. Here a pine announced, in red chalk, that it was three miles to the dam.

"Bowse ahead!" Fred exclaimed. "It 'll be pitch-dark before we get there!"

We walked and climbed on as fast as we could. It was a tolerably dry path, however; there were but two sloughs.

At intervals we could hear the roar of falls; but the path had diverged from the river, which comes down a ravine to the east of it.

The latter portion of the way was not so badly cumbered with fallen trees as we had found the first part, else we should have got quite discouraged. Nevertheless, dusk was falling over this whole wild region, and the deep recesses of the spruce woods had grown dark enough, when a turn of the path led us out to the brink of a great gorge, partially cleared of trees.

"Parmachenee!" shouted Fred.

The lake was not in sight; but we could plainly hear the ponderous plunge of the waters at the dam; and far down at the bottom of the gorge, near the foaming torrent, we could dimly discern a small log camp.

"Parmachenee at last!" Farr exclaimed. "Parmachenee gorge and camp!"

The path led down the side of the gorge, but it is amazingly steep and difficult. Half-stumbling, half-running, we made our way down. The old camp was of spruce logs, chinked up with moss and mud, and roofed as usual with "splits." It emitted a rather peculiar odor.

Like the camp above Escohos Falls, it contained a stove, — a very large, and withal a very rusty one, with an "elevated oven." There were two barrels of pork, a barrel of beans, about a third of a barrel of flour; tea, pepper, and salt in proportion.

These were the remains over and above the wants of the last logging gang. The stores had been standing here two years and over.

The flour was musty, the beans were *caked*, and the pork was in that rather precarious condition which Fred terms "sprung." When fried in a spider it frothed and foamed like a veritable wild boar; and the smell of it invariably put Scott to flight.[1]

We had no lamp or candles with us that night; and Fred had immediately set to work to provide a light, by frying some of the pork to get the fat for oil. This lard-oil he put in a pint-basin, then cut a button from his waistband, and through the holes in the button passed a bit of string for a wick. This contrivance for a burner he first floated on the fat, then lighted it; and lest the fat should cool and harden, he set the basin on the elevated oven of the stove. It burned well and steadily, giving a fair light.

We got our supper and ate it. Tired and hungry enough we had become.

As in the lower camp, there was a long bunk across the back side of the hovel. It was not without misgivings as to the possible population of the old fir-bough bed, that we turned in on it; yet we were too tired to get a fresh supply of boughs.

I sincerely hope that none of our readers have bethought themselves that the day now just passed in hard labor up the river, and harder tramping over the long carry, *was Sunday!* It is almost incredible as well as unpardonable that we had none of us thought of it. We had somehow, in the newness of the life we were leading, lost a day. I thought it was Saturday; so did the others. It was not till we were rolled up in our blankets that this irreverent fact came out.

Said Fred, "Let's see, how many days have we been getting up here? Started Monday; six days, is n't it?"

"Yes," said Scott. "First night down there in Grafton Notch, second at the Lake House, third at Moll's Rock, fourth in the old house below Escohos, fifth in the shanty above Escohos, sixth down there in

---

[1] It is customary for trampers in these wilds to help themselves to whatever stores they find in these old camps.

—why, fellows! — this is *the seventh night!* — ain't it? Hold on, let me count again."

We counted again; it was the seventh night, sure.

" Then to-day 's Sunday!" cried Scott, self-convicted.

" Can't be!" we exclaimed.

" Well, it *is!*"

" Blessed if it is n't, now!" admitted Fred.

" Well, I declare, we 're worse than a pack of heathen," I could not help saying. "We had better get a lath and make notches, if we can't remember better than this."

" What 's to be done?" said Scott, laughing in spite of himself.

" I don't see as anything can be done *now*," said Farr. " The day 's gone."

" Might keep to-morrow," I suggested.

My comrades reflected a moment.

" Oh, that would be mere fanaticism," said Scott, at length. " The only thing to be done is to try to remember better next time; for I believe in keeping the Sabbath as much as any one."

And so we went to sleep.

# CHAPTER XII.

FRED had potatoes nearly roasted in the "elevated oven" next morning before I was awake.

For our breakfast, we had roasted potatoes and butter, also a mess of Horsfords, — a bountiful mess, too, of which Fred exhorted us to partake largely. "For," said he, "we've got a tough day's work before us to get that boat up here and launched in the lake above the dam."

We had no doubt of that.

At a quarter of eight we set off to re-cross the carry, and climbing the side of the gorge, entered the path again. The woods were full of red squirrels, now in the midst of their morning antics; and so great a din did they keep up that little else could be heard. Scarcely had we gained the top of the ridge, however, when Farr espied three spruce partridges running in the path ahead of us. Scott had taken our little rifle. We fired at them and killed one, tearing a fearful hole through its body where the slug pierced it. Fred hung it up to a bough overhanging the path, that we might take it on our return.

About half way across the carry, Farr, who was ahead, suddenly drew up.

"Look here," said he, pointing to a large hoof-mark in the mud: "moose track. A moose has been along here since last night. Isn't that a moose track, Fred?"

Fred said it was one, for certain.

That was the first moose sign we had seen. The animal had walked along the path for some distance. The track was as large as the track of a large ox. Fred also pointed out to us where "saple" (marten) had dug in the moss in several places. These signs rejoiced us greatly.

"We'll have us a 'saple line' on both sides of the lake," Farr planned.

Just before coming out to the Little Magalloway, where we had drawn up our boat, we stumbled upon a second flock of partridges — five of them; Scott fired, but missed them.

At best, the bateau was a heavy boat, considered as a portable one. I do not know how many pounds it weighed, but should set it, for a guess, at four hundred; perhaps not more than three hundred and fifty pounds. There were four of us to carry it.

At first thought, this does not seem a very heavy load per man. But when the length and obstructed character of the carry are considered, I imagine that the reader will agree with me that we had anything but an easy job before us.

Two sticks were hewn from a fallen spruce, with handles at each end. These were not more than three feet long, and were nailed transversely, one across the nose of the bateau, the other across the stern, near each end, so as to allow the ends, or handles, to project far enough to take hold of. The boat was turned bottom up. It was then ready for carriage. We had only to take it up and go on.

Fred took the left-side handle at the bow. I took the other side, opposite him. Farr and Scott had the stern handles, the former on the right and the latter on the left. (We changed places afterward.) Farr carried the little rifle slung across his back. It was ten o'clock when we were at length ready for a start.

"Pick him up," was the word from Fred.

We picked *him* up. I for one was not in the least deluded in my first impression. It picked up heavy at the outset. I knew we had

THERE WERE FOUR OF US TO CARRY IT.

a big job on hand, and collected my strength, and tried to use it economically.

"We won't make long heats," said Fred. "We won't go more than twenty rods at once, without resting."

"That will make sixty-four heats for the four miles," Scott reckoned.

But as a matter of fact, we had nearly two hundred heats!

The path was barely wide enough to admit of our carrying it in the way that we had chosen. Often it grazed against the rough trunks on either side. And then the climbing over those countless windfalls across the path!

Ah, me! that is a task long to be remembered. We worked hard four hours, not including the half hour of rest we took at a little after noon. It was nearly three o'clock when at last we set the old thing down before the camp door.

Scott had passed through all the different stages of fatigue, from a profuse perspiration to a dry pallor. He went in without a word, and lay down in the bunk. We resolved to have something to eat, then carry the boat above the dam and launch it. For my own part, I felt as if I might drop at any moment, but determined to keep my legs as long as possible.

Fred made some strong coffee, and baked more biscuits and pota- toes. It came on dark before we had finished eating; so the boat lay over for next morning.

There is such a thing as being too tired to sleep well, or even at all. Scott did not go to sleep, he told me, till long past midnight. As for myself, I slept, but was still carrying the boat till toward morning, when a good nap succeeded.

But on getting up next morning, our stomachs were so lame that it was agony to draw a long breath or stoop. We were about used up, Scott especially; while Farr and even Fred complained a good deal of lameness and soreness. It made us wince and groan plentifully when we came to carry the boat up to the dam, — a hundred yards. Scott declared that it was like putting a knife betwixt his ribs to lift his side of the boat; and he came rather near profanity, on this wise: said he, " Do you remember what that hemlock down at the Forks said about the carry ? "

We did, distinctly.

" Well," says Scott, " I wish I *had let that stand as it was !* "

This peculiar mode of putting it set the rest of us laughing, but it · hurt us so horribly that our guffaws were speedily turned into howls.

The dam at the foot of the lake is built of spruce logs, and has five gates, set in ponderous hewn frames. There is a machine, consisting of iron cog-wheels and levers, for hoisting these. The dam itself is not more than a hundred and fifty feet in length. The site seems to have been very advantageously chosen. It has a perpendicular lift of about twelve feet. Brown, the agent of the Lumbering Company which owns the dam and the land about the lake, had told us the gates were up. We were, therefore, somewhat surprised to find three of them closed. Some one had either let them fall for mischief, or else to better the trout-fishing at the foot of the dam. The next day, before setting off up the lake, we raised the gates.

That forenoon, after launching the bateau, we unpacked some fishing tackle, — hooks and lines, — and taking pork for bait, went up to try our own luck at trout-fishing. There were several long alder-poles lying about on the dam. To these we attached our lines and dropped in. The trout did not rise to the pork bait readily; though after fishing for a half hour, Farr hooked a two-pounder. Fred meantime put on a red " fly," of which he had brought three from Upton. The trout rose to this in numbers, but would not *snap;* after fishing for some time, however, he caught one nearly as heavy as Farr's, and a few minutes after, a larger still. There were plenty of trout under the " apron " of the dam. We could see them rise, but the high water was unfavorable.

This was toward the end of the trout-fishing season. After the 15th of October the law protects them — as much as it can.

In the afternoon we went down the carry again, to get the remainder of our provisions and traps. (Scott, I should add, was left in the camp, to get over his lame stomach.)

We brought up this trip everything save the potatoes; and of these we had brought rather over a peck the previous evening.

Scott surprised us, and rendered us not a little uneasy, by announcing that he had seen a man — a rough-looking customer — up at the dam while we were gone down the carry. The fellow had a double-barrelled gun and, as Scott thought, a belt with a dirk-knife.

Immediately on catching sight of Scott down at the camp, he had made off. This looked suspicious; and fearing lest he might steal the boat, Scott took his gun and went up to the dam, in sight of where the bateau lay. But he saw nothing more of the woodsman.

This information disturbed us all a good deal, and Fred especially. He let out to us that the woods in this section of the State had borne a bad name, as being the resort of a gang of rough fellows, who had made the settlements too hot for them on account of various trespasses.

"But I was in hopes we should steer clear of them," he added.

For fear the boat might be stolen in the night, we went up, took it out of the stream, and brought it back to the camp.

There was something very unpleasant in the idea of being watched by such human beasts of prey.

# CHAPTER XIII.

## THE UPPER MAGALLOWAY.

THE next morning, as soon as it was light in the woods, Fred and I set off to bring up the potatoes.

Farr, meantime, took his double-barrelled gun and went off up the side of the outlet and lake to reconnoitre. We were desirous to know whether there was a gang camping anywhere about. By going up to "Loon Point," where the outlet leaves the lake proper, Farr thought he might detect the smoke, if there was a party at the head of the lake.

Scott remained in camp, partly as guard of our property there, and in part to recuperate and get better of his lamed stomach.

Fred and I got back up the carry at a few minutes before eleven. Farr had come in. He had seen no signs of a party; but he had run among a flock of partridges, of which he shot three at the first fire, and a fourth with his second barrel. And he had come upon the last August camp of a sporting party from New York City. A spruce told the story, to wit, that "R. Monheimer and party camped here from August 19 to September 3."

There was a raft drawn up near the camp. This party had not taken their boat over the carry, but had preferred to leave it down at the Forks, and build a raft for the lake.

Farr had poked about and found a pile of potatoes — nearly a bushel — at the foot of a tree, on which was written: "A free gift to whoever wants them."

They were, to use a young ladies' adjective, *splendid* potatoes, brought from Upton or Magalloway, probably, — localities noted for the excellence of their potato crop. The rains had washed them clean and white. Farr had at once determined to avail himself of Monheimer's offer. There was little doubt that we should want all the potatoes we could secure. After being brought all the way from Upton and "sacked" over the carry, they were very precious and really valuable.

Dinner was prepared and eaten. We then decided to set off for the head of the lake without further delay. That was the place where we wished to have our headquarters; and unless there was another party there, the sooner we took possession the better. And if there was another party there, we wished to find it out and keep clear of them.

The bateau was again carried up, put in the stream, and loaded with all our effects. We took from the supplies in the shanty a few pieces of the "sprung" pork, four quarts of beans, a paper of pepper, about a quart of salt in a box, and a small quantity of tea. These articles we thought we might need, and when we returned down the stream we could account for them to Brown; this is a customary procedure.

This done, we bade adieu to the camp in the gorge, and pulled off up the outlet above the dam.

Not more than fifty rods from the dam a large brook comes into the main stream from between two hills on the east side. An old trapper at Upton had told us there were beaver up this stream. We resolved to explore it ere many weeks, — after we got settled.

From the dam up to the lake proper at Loon Point, it is about a mile. This flowed portion of the outlet is a broad "thoroughfare," fifteen, twenty, and twenty-five rods in width.

We stopped at the Monheimer camp to take in the potatoes. It was just the place for a picturesque camp. No doubt Monheimer and friends enjoyed themselves. We were grateful for the potatoes.

On the east side of the outlet a forest fire had killed the growth far up the ridge. The dead trunks were falling across each other. It was a picture of vegetable ruin. Fire is the great devastator of our forests, and has destroyed more pine in Maine than all the lumbermen have cut off.

When near the lake, the outlet bends sharply to the west, around a bushy point. It was not till we had doubled this that the fine expanse burst on us. Farr had been up here already in the morning. I saw that he was watching the faces of the rest of us with a certain air of triumph.

"What say to this?" he exclaimed, as we rounded the bushes and caught sight of the lake.

Involuntarily we turned, and sat gazing off for a long time. This, then, was Parmachenee. I do not know what the name signifies, but it ought to mean "Beautiful Lake." The Indians named it; and I cannot but think, from the well-known fitness of their terms, that this silvery word has a beauteous significance.

It is not so large as Moosehead, Apmoogenamook, Umbagog, and a score of others; but to my mind it is the most beautiful of them all. Its whole length does not exceed five miles; and its greatest breadth, from the mouth of Moose Brook on the east shore to the foot of Bose-buck Cove at the southwest corner, is not more than four miles.

The most of our Maine lakes are long and narrow; Parmachenee is an exception. It fills a natural sink or basin, walled about by high, wooded hills, some of which are mountains of note. Bose-buck, for example, at the foot of the cove of the same name, is one of the finest cone-shaped peaks in New England.

Two hunters, with their dog Bose, were skirting the lake, — so the story has it. For some days they had shot nothing, and were suffering for food. As they passed the foot of the cove, Bose started a buck, which ran directly up the side of the mountain, till the dog overtook and pulled it down. So they named the peak *Bose's-buck*.

THE HOUSE WAS A SPRAWLING, ONE-STORY AFFAIR. — PAGE 57.

In the northeast, too, a very high blue mountain is visible over the nearer peaks. This is one of the Boundary Mountains. Over all the hills which border the lake shores, a heavy mixed growth comes down to the very water's edge, — spruce, birch, and maple, mainly, with here and there a grand old pine rising head and shoulders above everything else.

On the west side, above the cove, there is a grand slope, leading up from the shore for a mile, to the height of land.

"What a place for a farm!" Scott exclaimed, as we remarked it. "A fellow might make a paradise for himself on that slope! And what a view he would enjoy all his life long!"

There are no islands in the lower part of the lake. Toward the northern end, and above "Indian Field Point," there is a chain of three wooded islets extending down in a line; and above these there are numerous curious floating islands, some of an acre in extent, which rise and fall with the lake surface. They are covered with water-grass and a few low shrubs. These are the favorite haunts of the musk-rat; the islands are studded with their mud huts. The head of Parmachenee Lake is probably the best place for musk-rats in the State of Maine. But the poor little creatures are scarcely worth hunting; for some years their skins have brought no more than fifteen and eighteen cents, and often not over twelve cents. The afternoon was very pleasant. There was no breeze; the lake lay smooth as glass before us. A soft haze rested on the mountains, and the sunlight was mellow and warm. It was the poetry of October weather.

As we rowed on, we espied a very large flock of sheldrakes, and gradually approached them; but when within a quarter of a mile, they saw us and began to swim off. Fred took up the little rifle and fired after them. We could distinctly hear the whizzing of the slug, so still was the air. It struck a little short, and went skipping in among them, at which there was a prolonged quacking and flapping of wings; but they did not rise.

Reloading quickly, Fred fired again and again, without striking any one of the flock. It was not till the fifth or sixth shot that they rose. There were not less than fifty. They circled about for some minutes, then settled on the lake again at a distance of a mile or over.

We were nearly or quite an hour rowing up to Indian Point, which from the south side seems a part of the north shore, but which in reality separates the lake from a roomy expanse of a square mile or over, known as "Indian Cove."

We explored this cove pretty thoroughly, in search of the inlet where the Magalloway enters the lake. But the inlet is not through this cove, but off to the northeast. We at length got into it by passing in between the second and third of the wooded islands.

We had heard that there was a logging camp on the Magalloway at a little distance above the lake; and there we had had it in mind to take up our abode while at the lake. The stream enters the lake through a marsh full of black alder. It winds deviously about for a half mile or more. The whole upper end of the lake is in process of filling up with alluvial matter brought down by the river. Probably the lake occupied the whole space back to the woods formerly. But even after entering the woods, we found little current. There were long stretches of dead water.

The camp of which we were in search is located on the west bank of the stream, not quite a mile above the lake. Farr was the first to espy it.

"Here we are!" he sang out, pointing in past a great yellow birch trunk.

"Two camps," said Scott.

"One's the ox-camp," Fred explained.

"The other must be the man-camp," Scott reasoned.

We landed, to explore our prospective home. It was close upon the bank of the stream, — not more than twenty yards from it: a great ark of a camp, big enough to accommodate forty men, as thick as they usually stow them in a logging shanty. We were a little dismayed to find the roof broken in at one end. Heavy snows had done it. The end next the door was sound, however, for twenty feet or upwards.

"Well, there is enough of it left for us, as it is," said Fred, after we had surveyed the ruin.

This camp, unlike the most of them, had a double roof. Evidently it had been in its day a sort of palace among shanties. There was a floor of hewn planks, and a stove with two broken legs lying partially under the wreck of the roof.

There was also a grindstone, where the men sharpened their axes, and an anchor and anchor-line four or five hundred feet in length, used in warping rafts of logs down the lake.

In one of the logs in the end of the camp there were cut the words, "Cleaveland's Camp." This Cleaveland, Fred told us, had been a noted lumbering "boss" in this region.

We at once proceeded to set ourselves up in housekeeping in the habitable end of the camp. The roof had broken down in such a way as to keep out the weather, even from the ruinous end. It looked as if we might make ourselves comfortable. The old stove was extracted from the fallen splits, two stones substituted for its broken legs, and a hole cut through the roof for the bruised and battered funnel. It was not so good a stove as the one down at the Gorge camp; it did not "draw" so well, and it had no "elevated oven." As cooks, we liked "elevated ovens."

In order to have bait for our mink and otter traps, Fred and I went back down the stream to the lake (having first unloaded the bateau), to set traps for musk-rats on those floating islands where we had seen their huts.

In setting these traps for musk-rat, we took no pains to conceal or cover them; simply staked them down and left them uncovered, in the paths made by the rats.

On some of the islands there was a perfect net-work of these paths; and I counted not less than twenty huts. These latter are on the same plan as those of the beaver, only smaller and not so well finished. But the principle is the same. In both cases the entrance is from beneath and under water.

The musk-rat lives mainly on water-grass, roots, and twigs. It is not frequently seen out by day. We saw nothing of them, not so much as a glimpse, that afternoon. Asleep in their huts, perhaps.

Where the floating islands were of considerable extent, they bore our weight readily; but the smaller ones would begin to settle gradually deeper and deeper under the water, till we were glad to leap into the boat to avoid going over boots.

The upper end of the lake, above Indian Point, was a very curious place, with its floating islets covered with waving grass, and populous with huts, enclosed in a dark border of evergreen forest. By slightly magnifying the huts, in imagination, one could fancy that he had come upon some prehistoric settlement of the early human times, — a colony of rude lake-dwellers, living here in utter seclusion and harmony. We had invaded their long-secure retreat; and, alas! we were bringing nothing but war and death for them.

But such ideas have no business in the minds of trappers and hunters. We had come to slay for pay, — to get gain from it. A new and terrible destructive enemy had come upon the pigmy settlement, — an insatiable foe who would never rest till the last skin was in his bag.

We set sixteen traps, and went back to camp. It had clouded over, and begun to rain a little after sunset.

Farr and Scott had got everything under cover, and had the stove hot and supper cooking. For variety, Farr had stewed some beans and made a Johnny-cake.

Before the shower had begun to fall, Scott had brought in a great quantity of boughs, of both fir and spruce, for a bed. We drew the bateau out of the stream, so that it could not be stolen without our hearing something of it.

There were no signs of a party having been about the camp here, and we had seen nothing more of the prowling man at the dam.

" He may have been only some straggling hunter," Fred said.

In the ox-camp, which was placed about a hundred feet from the other, Farr had found as many as twenty axes stowed away in a grain box. This ox-camp was a dreadfully dirty hole, dark and stinking. It was roofed with sods and dirt to the depth of two feet. In winter it may have been warm, but now it dripped constantly.

As it grew dark, we heard the cries of many wild creatures, some near, some at a distance. The wilderness clearly had its dwellers. Night called them out. We were, as we now began to feel, in the very heart of the wild lands. Not a single human habitation within thirty or forty miles! If there were savage beasts in the forest at all, they were here, no doubt, and these were their cries.

From up the river the roar of falls came borne on the still air. The rain had ceased for a time, though it was very cloudy and the air was thick with mist. Objects had a wild gloom about them. We were not afraid, but this impression clung to us. Then there came the thought of the woodsmen, who had likely as not been observing our movements : this was the only real dread we experienced. The presence of man, or at least, of men of this sort, brought no reassuring feeling of companionship. So far from the settlements and the protection of law, crime knew no restraint. Deeds, however dark, could not be punished. Here we must look out for ourselves, and make our own rights good by force, if necessary. So used do we grow to the protection which the laws give us, that it is a bewildering thought to know, for the first time, that one is beyond their reach, and that his safety lies in his own strength and courage. At first it sends a strangely insecure feeling over a person ; afterward he comes to enjoy it and feel the freer.

There were plenty of owls here; and as the evening advanced we heard a loud snort, followed by others from the east bank of the stream. Scott took up the rifle, to fire in the direction of them.

"I don't believe I would fire," Fred said. "It will do no good, and it may do hurt. We had better fire no more than is necessary here."

Scott desisted readily.

We fastened our door securely. As for Spot, we could never get him out of the camp after dark; he was the most inveterate coward I ever fell in with — for a dog.

"DON'T FIRE!" SAID FRED.

# CHAPTER XIV.

## SETTING TRAPS.

FRED waked me early.

"Let's go look at our traps," he said. "We must be up early mornings, now. Time's precious. Farr and Scott can get the breakfast."

We launched the bateau and paddled down the river. The mist felt cold. It was barely light. There was frost on the wet dead leaves and on the water-grass. I shivered till warmed by the exercise of rowing.

Some creature swam the stream at a distance below us, and partially around a bend. We heard the splashing, but could see nothing distinctly. Fred thought it might be a deer, or possibly a moose. There was a snapping of brush as it ran off on the east side. Evidently there was game enough about, if we were smart enough to take it.

It is the dream of young sportsmen, particularly those from the cities, that in these wild regions game of all sorts is plenty, — so plenty that by just going out and walking for a few miles in the forest, deer, bears, and even moose can be frequently shot. But the fact is, that all these larger wild animals are exceedingly shy; and their senses are so acute that an amateur sportsman might hunt in these forests weeks together and never have even a glimpse of them. They hear, see, or smell, and are off long before he is aware of their presence. It is only by the utmost caution and by overmatching their natural keenness by successful stratagem, that game of this sort can be taken: this, at least, is the rule, though it sometimes happens that an animal is stumbled upon and shot in a manner most unaccountable to one who appreciates their natural shyness and acuteness.

It was with a good deal of expectation that we drew near the musk-rat colony on the floating islands. We could see them hopping about in the traps amid the grass, while yet at a distance.

" I set it at six," Fred said.

I thought four would be nearer the mark.

There were eight of them, hard and fast by the legs, leaping about and gritting their teeth. One was caught round the body and squeezed to death; it was a trap large enough for an otter. In two traps we found only *toes*. "Footed themselves," Fred said, meaning that they had gnawed off their legs to escape. Minks also do this frequently.

Some of the larger ones — the old male rats — jumped at us ferociously when we approached to *tap* them on the head; and when struck they uttered a curious squeak.

It seemed too bad; but then "business is business." With as little waste of time as possible we reset the traps, and pulled back to camp, keeping attentive eyes to everything stirring, or the least signs or sounds of game: this is the hunter's art.

Farr and Scott were up and getting breakfast.

Fred began to skin rats at once. I made "stretchers" for him out of the dry pine splits off the roof. We took the skins off whole, and immediately stretched them on the shingles, as I prepared them.

Skinning musk-rats, or any other sort of game, is work, not play, — very disagreeable work I call it. If the reader's nose has never realized the odor that a musk-rat emits while under the knife, he must imagine it, — that is all; for my own part, I should much sooner imagine it than smell it. But it is a job that has to be done, none the less.

We figured up our morning's profit at one dollar and twenty cents, reckoning the skins fifteen cents apiece.

This was our first profit, too; hitherto it had been all outlay.

It encouraged us and filled us with zeal. We believed we could make something, and determined to work; and from that time forward we did work. I never labored harder than during those weeks trapping and hunting at the head of Parmachenee. We got up early, and kept busy till dark; then skinned game till bedtime. We neither loafed nor played a moment that I can now recall. It was business, steady business, every hour.

As soon as breakfast was despatched we set off up the river, with traps and bait, to explore the falls, and put down mink-traps, if there were signs of mink.

It is rather over a mile up to the falls, — "Little Boy's Falls" they are called.

An Indian with his family were once crossing above the falls, when a pappoose tumbled off their raft, and was carried over. They got the little monkey out alive, however. Hence the name of "Pappoose," or, as it is more commonly called, "Little Boy's Falls."

It is a pretty fall of about six feet. The locality and the ledges which make the cascade are much like those at the Narrows.

A little below the fall there is a bark shed, built by some trapper, perhaps. It is only large enough to shelter two, at most. Past it runs a little brook, that flows into the stream from a pond only a few rods from the brook, — so near, indeed, that we drew out the bateau and carried it across to launch it, but were deterred by what we saw in the moss and in the sand on the shore. All along the water's edge the tracks of deer were as plenty as are sheep-tracks when a large flock have passed. Among these, too, Fred pointed to more than a score of great hoof-prints.

"Moose!" said he, in a whisper.

We carried back our boat without a word. It was a too promising

locality to be spoiled by premature hunting, or even by showing ourselves on the shore.

On the west side of the falls a bluff rises almost perpendicularly.
There are shelving rocks and many old roots with holes under them.
These holes were nearly all worn, as if by animals passing in and out.
Here we set five traps for mink, in the holes. We staked these, and
carefully covered them over with leaves and earth. The bait Fred
generally placed under the trencher, so that the animal would dig for
it through the dirt and leaves. The entrails of the rats were also
strung about, to make a scented trail to the traps. Fred had also
brought a bottle of the oil of anise, with which he *perfumed* the traps
themselves, to take away the odor of rusty iron, which both mink and
otter are quick to detect and instinctively avoid.

This occupied the forenoon.

In the afternoon we went off to set otter traps — we had four large
enough for otter — at a little pond to the west of the Cleaveland camp.
Farr had explored it the previous afternoon while we were setting for
musk-rat. He had found what he called two otter slides, and they
may have been such; the bank, indeed, was worn smooth, as if by
something sliding down it. We set two traps under water at the foot
of one of these, and another at the second. All three were chained
to poles such as trappers call "sliding-poles." If the otters should be
minded to slide here, we supposed that they might possibly slide a leg
into the traps. That was Farr's idea, at least.

Along the farther shore of this pond we saw, as at the pond above,
a vast number of deer-tracks. In some places the ground was trodden
hard; and there were occasional moose-tracks here, too.

In all our movements here we used care to make as little noise as
possible, and refrained from all loud conversation, and from firing the
guns.

It is a very easy matter to frighten off game from any given
locality. The more quiet the trapper keeps, the greater are his

chances for success. Animals do not readily leave their accustomed haunts, unless rudely scared. But a continuous discharging of guns will rout them in a very few days. This is especially the case with beaver, and to a less extent with otter.

The next morning we had seven musk-rats; and on going up to Little Boy's Falls we found that a mink had been in one of the traps, set in a hole under a birch root; but the trap had not held him, for some reason. We knew it was a mink, from the hair left on the trap-jaws. This was vexatious enough; for a mink is now worth from five to seven dollars, and mink were our great expectation.

The day after, and also Monday and Tuesday the following week, we were employed in setting up a "saple line" clean around the lake, — going down the east shore and coming back up the west shore, and keeping the height of land on the hills above the lake from half a mile to a mile back from the water.

The pine-marten is moderately plentiful in these forests, though rarely seen.

Fred tells me that one day while hunting near the Richardson Lake he sat down to rest on a stone, and a few minutes after saw a marten come out in sight, following his track. He had a bunch of partridges in his hand. The marten had smelled them, and followed him; but the instant it caught sight of Fred it vanished like a sun-ray, — before he could even cock his gun!

They are very shy little creatures.

Our "line" consisted of a hundred and thirty-one traps, in all, set at intervals of thirty-five and forty rods. These were all wooden traps, of the kind known as "dead-falls," "squat traps," "figure-four traps," etc. The entire length of the line was from fifteen to seventeen miles. It was a pretty good day's work to "go over the line," carry bait, reset such traps as were sprung, and carry home the game, if there was any. Then there was the drag to draw.

Two of us always went together on this round. It was not quite safe for one to go off alone for so long a trip, through such a wilderness, even if he was sure of getting round before dark.

To set up a hundred and thirty-one traps of this sort was something of a job, — as much as we could well do in three days, all four of us. Farr and Scott went ahead. At the place where it was desirable to build a trap they fell to work, and either cut up a quantity of stakes from saplings of the required length, — about two feet, — or else cut into the trunk of a fir or a spruce, and split out thick slivers to serve as stakes.

It was my duty to make the cuddy of the trap, by driving three stakes into the ground on three sides of a little square, a side of which would generally measure about fifteen inches. Besides the stakes, it was the duty of Scott and Farr to provide two poles for the " fáll," and two logs or heavy chunks of wood for weights. Fred brought up the rear, drawing the scented " drag " of musk-rat carcasses, and bringing the bait. He carried also a pine " split," out of which he made with his pocket-knife the spindle and " figure-four " arrangement. With him rested the care of the baiting and setting the traps ready for the martens. It was furthermore my duty to " spot " trees at intervals of a hundred yards along the whole line, in order that we might be able to follow it without difficulty in future.

There was an enjoyment from this work such as I cannot hope to make plain to the reader. It came to us out of the free, boundless forest, from the exercise itself, as well as from the hope of game to be captured. Yet were I to dwell on all these minor incidents the story might be deemed but a tedious recital. I can only urge the reader to bury himself for a few weeks in the woods, if he would experience it.

Down at the dam, too, and on the rapids below, we set eight or ten more traps for mink.

In the wooded valley above Mount Bose-buck on the west of the lake, and on the hard-growth slopes farther up, we found the partridges so plenty that a dozen could be shot by simply walking the "line." Never in any other spot have I seen them so numerous. This was about five miles below our camp; and we decided to do our bird-shooting here exclusively, within the compass of a couple of miles. The firing would not be heard at the head of the lake. A few martens might be frightened off ; but then we must have partridges.

During the time we were in camp there, I think we shot rising a hundred and fifty in all, the most of them over here among the hard-wood growth on this side of the lake. Sometimes we set off in the bateau on purpose to shoot partridges, but generally they were shot while making the round of the "saple" line.

While making these trips through the forest, we had kept a sharp eye to another possible source of profit, — to wit, spruce-gum. Farr had even dug a few pounds experimentally. On the ridge and mountain-sides where the spruce form nearly the entire growth, gum was to be found in abundance; of this fact we soon satisfied ourselves. There would be no great difficulty in digging a hundred-weight.

Rough gum was worth, we had learned, from seven to twenty cents a pound; but pure "purple gum," all cleaned and ready for chewing, would bring seventy cents, and even a dollar, a pound in the cities.

First we had resolved to try trapping and hunting thoroughly; then if game got scarce, we would go to digging gum, and make what we could from that.

For the week in which we set up the "saple" line we took forty-three musk-rats. I have little doubt there were a thousand of them about the little islands at the head of the lake.

Farr was the first to bring in a mink. He found it in one of the traps at Little Boy's Falls. How we doted over that slim mink! Almost black it was, with a beautiful gloss on its fur, and a tail that fairly glistened in the light of the basin-lamp, as Fred skinned it. This tail made to our eyes a very fine contrast with the bare snakelike tails of the musk-rats, of which we already had a long row hung up on one side of the camp.

"Good for six dollars," said Fred, as he hung it up to cure; "worth thirty-six of these rat-skins."

" Nearer forty," said Farr.  " It don't pay to trap rats, anyway."

Scott and I were the first to find marten in the traps.

Fred and Farr made the first round, the second day after we had set up the line.  They found nothing, and were not a little chapfallen.

But two days after, Scott and I found two martens on the east side and one on the west side of the lake.  Ah, that was a proud return to camp that night, — three " saple"!  It made Farr shout like a Methodist elder.

These martens were a third, yes, a half, larger than a mink. Over the back and sides their color was much like that of a fox. Beneath, they were a reddish white.  Their fur was very thick, and though lithe, they still had a chubby look, with the nose and head wonderfully slim, *sly*, and beautiful.

The tails were much more bushy than those of the mink.

Ah, there's no sport like trapping for youngsters of our age then!

We reckoned the three martens worth seven dollars and fifty cents.

That night, while sitting in the camp, eating supper, I think, we heard what sounded to me like the report of a gun at a distance. It startled us.

" Gun, was n't that? " Scott exclaimed.

" Gun, or a tree broke and fell."

" There's no wind," said Scott.

We were puzzled.

Farr thought it was a tree.  Fred declared he could not tell which it was.  The more we thought it over, the more readily we believed that it might be a tree.  But our first impression was that it had been a gun; and first impressions of such sounds are generally best.

FARR WAS THE FIRST TO BRING IN A MINK.

" I don't believe we had better leave our fur here in the camp days while we are off in the woods," Fred said, at length ; " or our provisions, either. It would be a very easy thing for some prowling party to come along and *go through us*."

We had planned to go up the stream above Little Boy's Falls the next day.

# CHAPTER XV.

## MOOSE-HUNTING.

EARLY the next morning, as soon as we had got breakfast under way, Fred carried the flour, meal, potatoes, meat, etc., off into a thicket at some distance below the camp, and covered them over with the tent and the rubber blankets. The fur he then hung up on the back side of the ox-camp. It was a dark hole in there; and Fred stood up old boards and piled up the grain-boxes in such a way that a person would not be very likely to see the skins, even if he went in. But our wool blankets and the tin-ware we did not think it worth while to remove.

Immediately after breakfast we set off in the bateau, pulled up to Little Boy's Falls, and cut a path through the bushes about them. Over this we carried the bateau and launched it in the stream above. It was a very short carry, — not over four rods long. We heartily wished all the carries were as short.

There is dead water for half a mile above, or at least the current is not strong. Then come short rips, where the stream is so very shallow that, had our bateau been loaded, we could not have got up. As it was, we had to lift it over two gravel bars. Generally there was water enough.

Two miles (for a guess) above the falls we came off abreast another camp with its ox-shed, — "Cleaveland's Upper Camp." This is the upper limit of logging operations. Above this point not even the omnipresent lumberman has penetrated.

At a place where there are black alder thickets bordering the stream, we saw a deer, but not in time for a shot. It had started to bound away before Fred espied it. We thought it was of the species known as caribou.

A more interesting matter immediately claimed our attention. A stick of hazel, green, and with the bark entirely peeled off, came floating down. Farr grabbed it out of the water. The ends were cut smoothly off.

"There's somebody not far above here!" he exclaimed. "This stick was n't cut many hours ago!"

"Let me look at that," said Fred, pulling in his oars.

We examined it carefully.

"That *somebody* is *beavers*," he said.

"Beavers!" Scott exclaimed. "Good!"

"Yes, fellows," Fred went on, looking critically at the stick. "See the mark of their teeth,—broad teeth? Hard telling it from a knife at first. But it's beaver, fast enough; done last night, too. May be a mile or two above here, though."

We pulled on, making just as little noise as possible, and speaking in whispers.

Presently we came to where the stream winds through a queer sort of tract, half open bottom, filled with wonderfully tall water-grass, and interspersed with thickets of alder and firs,—a place as singular in appearance as I ever saw. The stream here grew so narrow that our oars would sometimes stick in the banks on both sides, but the channel was very deep, with little current. And here, at a place where some thick and shaggy firs leaned out from the banks, just after turning a bend, we came upon the beavers' own retreat! There were no houses, but the bank around the firs was worn and trodden smooth where it fell off into six or eight feet of water; and the stream had undermined the roots of the trees. All the hazel and alder bushes near the bank had been gnawed off, and the ground was covered with bare sticks. Many of these were floating about.

"They live under that bank," Fred whispered.  "Bet you there are half-a-dozen of them!"

A little above, we saw where they had felled a poplar, six inches across, so as to have it fall out into the stream.  The small branches of this were completely denuded of bark.

During the summer and early fall, beavers are seldom found at their winter houses.  They wander about in families, and occasionally solitary individuals, visiting many different streams over a considerable territory, till ice begins to form, when they once more seek their homes.

We supposed this to be some such family which had taken up their abode under this quiet bank for a few weeks.

We had taken along our one large trap.  This we attached to a sliding-pole and set it on the bottom under the bank.  Quietly then, and without a loud word, we pulled away and continued our cruise up-stream.  We had heard of a pond somewhere on the upper waters of the stream.  Lumbermen called it "Rump Pond," — a reference to venison, perhaps.  We hoped to reach this pond that day.

We passed the mouths of numerous brooks, and indeed the main stream showed unmistakable signs of dwindling to a brook itself.

About an hour later, I judge, and after pulling perhaps five miles above Little Boy's Falls, we *crooked* our way into a pond, which I doubt not is the "Rump Pond" above mentioned.  It was a rather pretty expanse of perhaps a square mile in extent, set about with the usual evergreen forest, and showing the tops of dark peaks over the woods, at a distance.

There is a pleasure in exploring wild and unknown ponds and streams.  Something of this we felt as we pulled out of the river and saw this new pond spread out before us.

In order to thoroughly explore it (from a trapper's point of view), we went up the west shore, looking for mink and other signs, intending to return down the east shore.

There are on the west side several little coves where small brooks make in. Into the second of these, with noiseless dips of the paddles, we were just turning, when we heard distinctly several leisurely splashes, as of a cow walking in a pool, just within the cove and around a thick bunch of black alders.

"Sh!" from Fred.

Instantly we reversed the stroke.

Scott was in the bow. He peeped with eyes round as a lynx's, but the alders were too thick. Fred crawled along beside Scott. They both peered eagerly. Then Fred's hand dipped cautiously in the water and paddled us imperceptibly forward a yard or more; both staring intently all the while, with Farr and myself craning our necks for a glimpse, one hand on our guns.

Suddenly Fred started and ducked his head. I saw his hand feeling behind for his gun.

"Moose!" he breathed to us behind his other hand.

Farr's eyes glistened. I presume my own fairly snapped with excitement. But every other second, Fred would turn us just the white of one of his, warningly and beseechingly. As for Scott, he had caught sight of the game at last, and stared rapturously, never once winking, and evidently quite forgetful of the rifle.

Farr and I could not stand this. We were expiring for a look. We began to crawl forward, regardless of the prayers in Fred's eye. Seeing us coming, he cocked both barrels, and hearing the faint clicks, Scott grabbed for his own rifle; he had just thought of it.

"Look, if you must," Fred aspirated.

Like two clumsy snakes, Farr and I crawled over the thwarts and partly on to Fred. Our four heads were now all in the bow; we were all eyes then. Ah! but was n't that a picture for a hunter's optics!

Up in the cove, close under a bunch of swamp maples that hung out over the water, and standing knee-deep among reeds and pickerel grass, and all in the shadow of the tall dark firs behind, there they stood, two of them.   Perhaps it was sixty yards ; not over that.   They had not heard us, or at least they had not seen us.   I could think of nothing but two great donkeys, or rather, two enormous rabbits. Neither of them had antlers, but they had prodigious flapping ears. They were nosing the water and the grass ; and as I looked, the larger raised its ungainly nose and with its muffle and teeth cropped the twigs of the swamp maple.   They looked to me quite black, where they stood, and seemed grotesquely ugly, — ungainly in every part, as we appreciate beauty.

But poor Farr had not yet got a good look.   I doubt if he had even got his eye on them, through the alder-brush.   He made a fresh effort to get farther forward, on to Scott ; and in so doing, he hit his toe against the tin bailer in the bottom of the boat.   It rattled.

"You 've done it now!" Fred whispered in disgust.

Instantly both moose started sharply, raising their huge ears.   For an instant they stood cowering, — trembling, I fancied, — their great eyes dilating toward the alders.

"Fire, Scott," Fred whispered.   "Let drive!"

*One !* spoke the little breech-loader.

A loud snort! A mighty splashing !   *Bang — bang:* both barrels of Fred's gun.   I had a long single-barrel, and fired the same moment through the smoke at what I took for the moose, — one or both, — and Farr let fly both barrels of his shot-gun, at random necessarily.   There was a smash of brush, a jar and pounding of the ground. Almost at the same instant a singular sound, twice repeated, such as I once heard a young elephant at a menagerie make through his trunk.

"Pull in !   Pull in !"   Fred shouted.

Under our excited strokes the bateau forged into the cove and plunged through the reeds into the muddy bank.   We jumped out and looked for traces.   There were deep hoof-prints in the soft black muck.

THE WOUNDED MOOSE MAKING FOR WATER.

The water was turbid with mud; and on the slime and beaten-down weeds there was a tinge of blood.

"Some of us hit!" Farr exclaimed.

"And look here!" said Fred.

On the round withered leaf of an orchis there stood a bright red drop, and against the trunk of a fir another had spattered and run down; and still farther up the bank another had splashed on a white birch.

"Blood flew well," said Scott; "but they're gone."

Fred was hastily reloading. Farr and I followed his example. Whether one or both were seriously wounded, we could only guess. They had gone out of sight and hearing.

"Too bad we left Spot," Fred said; for lest he should bother us, by eating bait or frightening game, we had left him shut into the camp that morning. Spot was not a good trapping dog; he had little knowledge of anything save of his own wants. It was a mistake from the outset taking a dog; but just now he might have been of use.

The prints of their hoofs were plainly visible, however, on the dead leaves. We followed in hot haste. Blood-drops here and there encouraged us. For a considerable distance — a mile, very likely — the moose ran off up from the pond shore to higher land. They were keeping together. At places where the ground was moist we tracked both of them. The direction must have been west or northwest; though we paid little attention, in our excitement. Soon, however, the trail veered; the moose had tacked for lower ground again.

"Making for water!" panted Fred.

We ran on, in better hopes.

"Good sign," Farr said.

But we were in nowise certain that they were going for water.

A hundred rods farther on we entered a great alder bottom full of grass, bushes, and cat-tails. Here there was a very distinct trail; but it was slow work beating through the undergrowth. Tearing ahead, we came out upon a big brook, and almost at the same moment heard a crash of twigs, a snort, then another of those trumpeting squeaks. Fred was ahead.  He fired.

"One of them!" he shouted.  "Gone like a streak!  Come on."

We jumped into the brook waist-deep, splashed through it, and were climbing up the bank, when Farr stopped short.

"Why! see there!" he exclaimed, pointing into the brush and water in the bed of the brook, a few yards above where we were crossing.

What seemed a great mass of wet hair and hoofs lay half under water!

"By Jove!" cried Fred.  "*If there is n't the moose!*"

There it lay, sure enough, flat in the brook, dead as a stone!

The thing astonished us.  After drinking, it would seem to have fallen dead in the water.  The other had stayed about till we came up.

Farr thought that the smaller one was a calf; for this one that we had shot was a cow-moose.  For my own part, I had not detected much difference in their size.

Fred was not at all sure that he had hit the second one.  We could see no blood; and after looking along for twenty or thirty rods, we gave it up; we felt very tolerably content.

This larger brook, as we began to suspect, turned out to be the upper course of the main stream above the pond.  It was not over twenty feet wide here, with many sharp crooks, but the depth was not much under two feet at any place; for the current was sluggish through the alder swamps.

As soon as we had satisfied ourselves that the brook was the inlet of the pond, we determined to take out the moose in our boat.  The carcass was so heavy that all four of us could scarcely raise it.  We judged it might weigh toward seven hundred pounds.  Farr and Scott set off to take the bateau up the brook; while to avoid carrying a heavier load than necessary, Fred opened the carcass to take out the entrails.

Wishing to be able to state the actual size of the moose, I carefully measured its length, as it lay on the bank, with the tow-line, and indicated the measurements by knots. The entire length, from the roots of the tail to the end of its muzzle, was (as I afterward verified it by a rule) eight feet three inches. Its height, from the tips of its forward hoofs to the top of its withers, was six feet and an inch. Its girth about the body, just back of the forelegs and shoulders, was five feet and eleven inches. This was a cow-moose, it must be borne in mind. The male is said to be often a third larger.

Scott and Farr were fully two hours getting the bateau up the stream to where the moose lay. And the getting back down to the pond with the heavy carcass aboard was a still longer task. We had to lift the boat over logs and " jams " of brushwood, wading ourselves nearly the whole distance with our hands on the gunwale.

# CHAPTER XVI.

## AN UNPLEASANT MYSTERY.

AT the portage, on getting down to Little Boy's Falls, we had another stint. The moose was much heavier and more unwieldy to carry across than the bateau; indeed, we did not carry it, but dragged it perforce.

These labors consumed the time. It was after sunset before we were clear of the falls; and dusk was falling as we drew near the camp.

We had, I recollect, turned the "big crook" and entered the long stretch of dead water that led down past the camp, when Farr stopped paddling, and sniffed, quite on a sudden.

"Don't you smell smoke?" he exclaimed.

We all sniffed, at that.

There was a very perceptible odor of resinous smoke.

"Pine burning," Fred said.

We looked at each other in great uneasiness; then began to paddle in haste.

"You don't suppose —" Scott began.

"Yes, sir!" Fred cried out, standing up in the boat as we came down past the last thicket on the bank. It *is* the camp! Burnt up!"

Where the camp had been there was a bright bed of coals and smoking logs!

The suddenness of this catastrophe, coming so closely on our good luck, struck us quite speechless.

"Poor Spot!" Scott exclaimed, breaking the silence of our dismay.

"Burned up with it," said I.

But Spot was not dead. A moment later we caught sight of him standing out near the ox-camp; and hearing our voices he came to meet us, limping, and with a blood-stain on the white hair just back of his left shoulder. He wagged his tail in a sad sort of way when we spoke to him. His whole appearance and manner seemed to say, — "We've had an awful time here!"

Landing hastily, we went to look at the ruins. Not much to be seen, — only coals and a few logs not wholly burned. Evidently the fire had taken place some hours before. "What will Brown say to this!" Fred exclaimed. "Camp's gone."

"But I don't see how it caught," Farr said. "We left scarcely a spark of fire in the stove, and I shut it up close and tight the last thing before I came out."

"Well, there it is — in ashes," said Fred. "Of course it must have caught from the stove somehow: a coal may have snapped out, and got down between the planks of the floor, while we had our fire going for breakfast. But I don't see how Spot got out! Here, Spot; come here. He does not seem to be singed!"

"Oh, he dug out somehow," said Farr. "You weren't going to stay in there and be burned up, were you, old fellow?"

Spot looked volumes, but said little.

"And our blankets!" said I.

"And all our plates and kettles and things!" Scott exclaimed.

"Lucky we took out our fur," Farr said, "and our potatoes and flour."

Fred ran down to the thicket where he had hidden the provisions. "Yes, they are all right," he said, coming back.

Farr went out to the ox-camp to look to the skins.

"And there was that great grindstone and anchor and anchor-line,"

·Scott anxiously enumerated.  "Why, Brown will raise Cain with us for letting this camp burn!"

Fred was looking among the coals and logs.

"I don't see a sign of the stone or the anchor," he said.  "Now, is n't that queer?"

"Under the ashes and coals," Scott suggested.

"But there lies the old stove," said Fred; "it does n't seem to be broken up much, either."

Suddenly Farr called to us from the ox-camp.

"Just come out here!" he said.

We ran out.

"Fur gone?" questioned Fred, anxiously.

"No; the skins are just where you put them," Farr said.  "But look in here!"

There was a small side shed joining the end of the ox-camp, where they kept the grain and other provender in great boxes.  The door had a huge wooden button on it.  Farr had opened it, and stood pointing inside.  We took a hasty look within.  *There lay the anchor-line and the anchor; and there stood the grindstone!*

"Did you bring those things out here this morning before we went off?" Farr queried.

"Why, no!" Fred exclaimed.

"No, indeed!" said Scott and I.

"Well, somebody has," Farr replied.

We felt confounded at this.

"Somebody was here when the camp burned, and took these things out," Farr repeated.

"And set the camp afire themselves!" Fred exclaimed.

"But I can't understand this at all," Scott said.

"Well, I can," said Fred.  "You see, there's some one — half-a-dozen, perhaps — lurking about.  They came along here to-day, and found us gone.  Like as not they are trapping themselves not far off.

They want to drive us off; so they set the camp afire. But I suppose they thought it was rather too bad to burn up that anchor-line; it's worth forty or fifty dollars. Perhaps they mean to use it themselves; so they carried that and the anchor and grindstone out here."

" But how about our blankets and tin-ware?" I said.

" Oh, they have stolen those," said Fred.

" And Spot?" Farr queried.

" I'll bet they tried to kill him," said Fred.

" Shot at him or struck him. Poor doggy! Did they try to murder you, Spot? But you got away from them, did n't you?"

We looked at the bloody stain on his back again. There seemed to be a cut through the skin; but it did not look like a shot-mark. We could only surmise how he received it, or with what sort of a weapon.

And explain it as we would, the whole affair was more or less a mystery: there was something queer about it. Whoever had been there in our absence, they had left no trace; yet we knew that somebody must have been there.

" Well, shall we bring up the tent, or camp here in the grain-shed?" Fred at length asked; for it was growing dark.

As the grain-shed was a very comfortable little shanty, we decided to bunk in it, and use the tent in place of our wool blankets, that had been either stolen or burned. The only objection to this arrangement was that it was rather too near the ox-camp; but we were not over-fastidious.

Among the ruins I found the long-handled spider; but the potato-kettle was broken in halves, and the other had a big crack through it. Nevertheless, Fred cut some large thick slices of moose-meat to fry; and our potatoes we roasted in the hot ashes and coals of the burned camp. We also scraped together a great heap of the coals, and cooked large " hunks " of the moose sirloin in a still more novel manner: we thrust them through with a sharpened stick of green maple, and then setting one end of the stick in the ground, let the meat hang over the coals, a foot above them.    It cooked nicely so.    It was fine eating. Despite our vexation at the loss of the camp and our blankets, and the continual feeling of anxiety as to who and what were plotting mischief about us, we yet enjoyed that supper of moose-meat.    We were hungry; and it was superlatively good.

The hide we carefully took off the carcass, and hung it up as a trophy of our first moose.

THE HIDE WE CAREFULLY TOOK OFF THE CARCASS.

# CHAPTER XVII.

## CHANCE SHOTS.

AFTER what had happened, we decided to keep guard in future, not only by night, but by day. That night we watched each two hours, in turn, as also the next night. It would have been much better for us to have stuck to this rule, as it turned out. But after three nights, we knocked off watching, and all slept, as before.

By day, however, we did not leave the camp unguarded. One of us always stayed about, with a loaded gun; and this considerably interfered with our work, too; though Fred used to sometimes make a round of the "saple" line alone. None of the rest of us went off so far alone. It did not seem quite safe. Besides, seventeen miles through the woods alone is not a pleasant ramble.

The next day after the burning of the camp Farr and Scott went down the lake to the camp in the gorge, after tin plates, knives, forks, etc. We found it quite impossible to keep house without something of this sort; and save the frying-pan, we had lost our whole kit; for which, I may here add, we had to give Godwin a six-dollar mink-skin in payment.

That day I watched the camp — with Spot. Fred went over the line alone. I had the little rifle and one of the double-barrelled guns all loaded and ready. I kept inside the grain-shed the most of the time, and turned it into a fortification by cutting loop-holes through the sides. If any of the supposed marauders came near I meant to cover them through a hole with the rifle, and bid them stand and give an account of themselves; and if their account was not satisfactory, I meant to bid them begone in a terribly bass voice. In fact, I even practised a vocal series of "begones!" and "clear outs!"

If they did make an attack on the shed, I fancied I could make it hot for them.

We felt terribly warlike for a few days after the fire; we missed our blankets considerably nights, and had it not been for the tent we should have lain cold indeed.

At night we talked of little else save what we should do if we were attacked, or found any of them about the camp.

For this week, we took thirty-four musk-rats, three more martens, and toward the last of the week, a mink at the falls; and on Sunday following, a mink got into one of our traps below the dam at the foot of the lake. Farr and Scott found it there the next morning. But nothing was taken in the otter traps, nor yet in the trap we set for beaver up near Rump Pond.

We watched two nights for deer at the pond, off to the west of Little Boy's Falls, but did not get a shot.

On the following Wednesday Farr made a remarkable chance shot. He had got in the habit of loading his shot-gun — one barrel of it — with the bullets he had run for the old Sharpe's carbine, the one that burst at Bottle Brook Pond. The shot-gun had a large bore, and he used (whether prudently or not, I shall not attempt to say) to put in two and three of these bullets, with a handful of shot to keep them steady, and powder enough to throw them. This barrel, thus loaded, he kept for emergencies, doing his ordinary shooting with the other barrel.

Wednesday afternoon we set off in the bateau, Farr, Scott, and I, to shoot partridges down at the slope on the west side of the lake.

We had doubled Indian Field Point, and were making our way down the shore, keeping close in, when Scott espied something moving a long way ahead of us. It was an animal standing partly in the water and in the shadow of the spruces, which there leaned out over the lake. Scott spoke to us of it. We stopped rowing; but he had some trouble to make us see it, the distance was so great.

I cannot say just how far off it was, but do not believe it to have been under fifty or sixty rods. Farr at length got his eye on it, and stretching out at full length in the bow, took aim and fired the three balls and shot at it.

Instantly the creature turned, bounded out of the water, and went out of sight into the woods. Scott and I laughed; so did Farr.

"We might have got a little nearer," Scott said, humorously.

We had no thought that the creature was hit. It took us some little time to get down where the animal had stood. We passed close to the shore, to see the track.

"It was a deer," said Scott, after a glance at the small hoof-track in the mud.

"I will just get out and take a look," he added, jumping ashore.

He went up the bank, and was gone not more than three seconds when we heard him shout, — "Farr, you killed it deader than a nail!"

We both jumped out at that, and ran up the bank.

There, among a clump of round-wood, lay a small deer, with its tongue out and one fore-leg in the air, dead. One of those bullets had gone through its body, striking just in front and beneath its left hip, and coming out near the right shoulder. 'T was a purely chance shot, I suppose, but a very lucky one, certainly. Farr felt not a little proud of it; though he owned that it was mere luck.

We did not trouble to go farther after partridges that afternoon.

This was not a caribou deer, but one of the ordinary species (*Cervus Virginianus*). We judged it to have been a last spring fawn; its color was unusually light for the species, and it was seemingly not more than half grown. It would not have weighed over seventy-five pounds undressed.

Again we revelled in venison ; but the meat did not have the body and flavor of the moose meat.    This latter was equal in quality to the best of beef, and to our palates (while up there) far superior in flavor.

I think it was the next morning after shooting the fawn, that Spot came in while we were eating breakfast, with his nose full of hedgehog quills.    In his morning stroll through the woods he had stumbled on a "quill-pig," as Fred terms them.    To get out these quills Farr made a pair of wooden pincers, by splitting a blunt stick of dry ash at one end.    With this he pulled out the most of them ; but we had to hold the dog down by main strength to do it.    Next day his nose was badly swollen, and so sore he would not eat.

It would appear that there are hedgehogs in this northern forest, though we did not see one.

Not more than two mornings after, we had a very lively adventure with a wild-cat, or lynx.

It was Scott's turn to guard the camp that day.    Fred, Farr, and myself had gone down to the dam to look to the traps there and on the rapids below.    We were coming back up the outlet toward the lake, when, quite suddenly, a great snapping of twigs and racing through dry brush began up among the dead growth on the east side, where the fire had run some years before.

" Hark !" Farr said.    " What's that ? "

It was about the liveliest snapping and scampering I ever heard. It went *tearing* along the ridge-side.    Presently there was a sound of nails in the bark of a tree ; and we saw, first, a marten run up a dead hemlock, in sight from the stream, over the other trees.    After him came a largish gray animal with a big head.

" Lucivee ! sure 's ye live ! " Fred muttered, under breath.

The marten ran up to the very top of the hemlock ; but the wild-cat durst not trust himself on the fragile topmost limbs.    He came to a stop while yet eight or ten feet below the marten, and clung, glaring at it.

IT MADE A FLYING LEAP OF TWENTY-FIVE OR THIRTY FEET.

Farr cocked his gun.

"No, no," Fred whispered; "too far! Pull in ashore. We can work up through the woods. Sh! still!"

Landing, we ran up toward the hemlock. The place was full of dry brush. It snapped, despite our care. Yet so intent was the lynx on its prey that it did not stir nor turn its eyes from the marten, though we came within a hundred yards.

"I can drop him from here," Farr said.

"Well," said Fred, "I'll take the 'saple.'"

They both fired.

The marten leaped instantly into another tree, a dead poplar. 'Twas a long jump, — not less than thirty feet off, and downward. The dry branches among which it caught broke. Down it came, snapping and crackling, to the ground, but instantly ran away like an arrow.

But our attention was mainly directed to the big cat. As Farr fired, he turned a pair of great staring eyes on us, then whirled about and ran down the hemlock. We sprang forward, shouting loudly; but it reached the ground and ran. Before it had taken three jumps, however, I let go at it with the single-barrelled gun. I don't think I hit it; but the report and the shouting so frightened the creature that it took to the trunk of a large green hemlock standing near, and went up amid the green boughs in a trice.

"We've got him now," Fred exclaimed. "Surround the hemlock. We'll pepper him. We'll have some fun now!"

Reloading the guns we walked round the hemlock at a distance from the roots, peering into the green top, to get a glimpse of the animal. But so dense were the boughs, and so snugly had the beast ensconced himself, that we none of us could get eyes on him. The tops of these great hemlocks are often surprisingly thick. Whether the lynx was up near the top, or midway the tree, we could not tell.

"Let fly up the trunk," Fred at length said to me. "Farr and I will stand ready to nail him, if he jumps out."

I went up to the foot of the hemlock, and fired up into the top a charge of heavy duck shot. Possibly some of these hit the animal. Instantly it jumped out of the top and made a flying leap, with its legs spread out, of twenty-five or thirty feet, to the ground. Fred and Farr both fired. The beast struck the ground with an audible *thump*, but at once regained its legs and went off at full jump. Farr aimed and fired his second barrel, the only effect of which was to make the brute take a prodigiously high leap, and run the faster.

Without stopping to load, we ran after it, shouting and yelling at the top of our lungs, in the hope of driving it up another tree. But we soon lost sight of it; and though we chased on for forty or fifty rods, we saw nothing more of it. 'T was quite a lively sort of scrimmage; though nothing came of it.

We got a mink down at the dam that morning. It had gnawed its leg almost off. In ten minutes more it would have been free — to run on three legs. Determined little chaps, these minks!

# CHAPTER XVIII.

A DAY or two after, we took up our large trap, up at the "beaver bank," and set it in a "bear path" which Fred had crossed about a half mile to the west of the pond near Little Boy's Falls. Fred was a great case for hunting up signs of game. Often he would go off for an hour or two and search steadily for paths, tracks, croppings, and dens. I think he discovered five or six dens of bears. The trouble with these dens is, to tell whether there is a bear in them or not; and if there is, to get him out without too great personal peril.

This trap was hardly large enough to hold a large bear; yet it might hold a small one, we reasoned. So we set it with great care and preparation in a bed of dry leaves, at a place where the path wound between several large rocks. We took along an abundance of bait: musk-rat carcasses, moose bones, and refuse pieces of meat. These we scattered about and placed upon the rocks. Entrails of the musk-rats we strung about. Directly over the trap we bent down a sapling and hung on it a big piece of moose meat. Altogether we provided a feast of it.

"Should think that might draw a crowd," said Farr, pausing for a final inspection of the arrangements.

We did not chain the trap, but attached to it a couple of heavy clogs off a spruce trunk.

Fred ran over to see if there was anything caught in it the next morning. There were, he told us, no signs of there having been any animal about it.  So we let two days pass before looking to it again. Indeed, it was the afternoon of the second day after that, when Fred and I went over to it.  Farr had gone up to the falls, and Scott was on guard with Spot.

This time we found nearly all of the bait eaten up, and the trap gone, clogs and all.

Through the moss and on the dead foliage there was a very distinct trail where the clogs had torn along.

"What is it, suppose?" I queried.

"Bear, or a lucivee," said Fred, looking to the caps of his gun.

I had the little rifle.

We followed the marks in the moss and leaves, keeping a cautious eye ahead.  We did not care to run upon the beast unawares.

It did not seem as if the creature could have dragged those clogs very far.  But we followed a mile, perhaps more, without seeing anything of it, and began to think it might prove a long chase.  Night was coming, too.  The sun had not been more than an hour high when we set off.

Not a great way farther on, however, the trail entered a swamp full of hackmatack and alder.  This swamp bordered on a large, unknown pond.  We presently came out in sight of it.  Fred was ahead.  Suddenly he stopped and backed hastily against me.  At the same moment I heard a growl.

"Behind that old log!" Fred exclaimed, still backing off.  "Look out! he may make a dive at us!"

We cocked our guns and stood on the defensive.  The creature's ears were just in sight over the log: it was crouching there.  Fred picked up a stray knot and pitched it over the log.  In a moment the old fellow rose up, and the way he screeched at us was lively to listen to!

'T was a lynx.  He drew up his gray back, cat-fashion; the hair stood up.  His prick ears lay back felinely; and his big eyes shone

FRED SHOULDERED IT AND STARTED.

like silver knobs. Oh, he looked ugly! No doubt he felt ugly. Evidently a fight was what he most longed for, — a regular set-to with teeth and nails. He seemed to say, "Come on, if ye dare! I'll slit your cowardly hides for ye!"

But we had not a moment's time to lose. Darkness was coming.

"Let him have it!" said Fred. "Right between the eyes!"

I took aim with the rifle and fired.

A yelp followed the report. The creature turned and ran, dragging the trap. The slug had struck the skull a little too high, as we saw afterward, and glanced along the bone betwixt its ears.

Fred ran on after it with his gun half raised to get a shot. The clogs impeded the animal so much that after a few rods it sprang to the butt of a great hackmatack, and assayed to climb up; but the clogs were too heavy. It got up five or six feet and stopped; it could not raise the clogs from the ground.

Fred ran forward, and taking a rapid aim at the back of its head, fired a barrel of his heavy shot. Down it dropped, the trap rattling and clogs flying about. In a few seconds it was dead.

Fred took it out of the trap as soon as it stopped kicking. It was caught by one of its hind legs.

The lynx is a very furry animal, and looks much larger than its weight would bespeak it. This one we thought would not weigh over thirty-five or forty pounds, although it looked as large as a rather large dog. Its head was very large.

We did not dare to stop to skin it there, lest it should come on so dark that we might not be able to find our way back to camp. So Fred shouldered it and started.

I threw off the clogs from the trap and followed him. It was dark enough, too, before we got back to camp. Farr and Scott had begun to feel pretty uneasy about us.

This was a male lynx. The fur was in tolerably good condition: a stone gray on the back and sides, but almost white beneath. Its legs were very powerful and muscular; its feet were padded with thick fur. We cut and pulled out several of the claws to save for mementos. Those from the middle toes of the fore-paws were an inch and a half long. The teeth were much sharper and rather longer than those of an ordinary dog. (We compared them with Spot's.) The tail was very short and tipped with black hairs.

If I remember aright, we received three dollars and a half for the skin, sold with the rest of our fur.

# CHAPTER XIX.

## CAPTURED BY OUTLAWS.

IT was the night after this capture, — the night of the 29th of October. Ah, I shall never forget that night! There had been a snow-squall the previous afternoon. We had got in early from looking to the traps. The stove we moved into one end of the grain-shed; for the weather was getting rather chilly nights, as well as windy days. A glorious supper of partridges and deer venison cheered us. We kept the stove hot and lay on a great springy bunk of boughs, with our rubber blankets and the tent for coverlets.

Our sleep was sound after those days of constant toil and tramp through the forest.

Over our heads, as we lay, hung five mink-skins and three marten pelts. But all our musk-rat and the lynx skin and moose hide were out in the ox-camp, hidden there behind the boxes and boards.

The night passed. It was faintly daylight, and very nearly our usual time of getting up, when I was waked by Spot barking savagely — for him.

I jumped up, bewildered and greatly alarmed, with the sense of something being around the camp. The other boys were rousing, too. But before any of us could get fairly up, or reach the guns, the door was kicked open, with loud, fierce shouts, which were more like the savage growls of wild beasts than men; and the muzzles of two guns were pointed in at us as we sat up in the bunk! At the same instant we saw red, bearded, vicious faces peeping rather cautiously in! And I still think had we seized our guns promptly, the cowardly wretches would have fled even then. They might have discharged their guns, which might, of course, have hit some of us. But they were cowards, as such scamps often are.

We were just simply stunned: we were hardly awake; and then their brute-like shouts appalled us.

"He-air, yar young ——! Af yar star, we'll blaw yar ter ——!" one of them yelled at us, with a guttural rattle and rasp in his throat, keeping the gun pointed full in our faces, and creeping through the door-way like a tiger, the others after him.

Such sounds I never heard from men. They drew back their lips like mad dogs, and snarled, gritting their teeth, the front one especially. "*Sacré! Sa-a-a-cré! Sacré! Sa-a-a-cré!!*" he growled out, more than a score of times. He had a gray fur cap on his head. His hair hung down long; his face was red and dirty. His coat or frock was of skins. Even in the terror of the moment, I smelled a vile stench of rum. Altogether, he was the most terrible object I ever saw in human form — or out of it. They swore awfully, — a continued stream of the most frightful and disgusting profanity, and all with the unmistakable accent of French Canadians. But they knew a good deal of English. Indeed, one or two of the gang were English, or Americans, at least.

"Af yar star! Af yar star!!" the leader kept snarling at us.

Of course we were frightened. Who would n't have been? We expected to be murdered. They looked capable of it. And they had us in their power. If we had so much as moved to take up a gun, they would have shot us. There were five of them. Instinctively the rest of us glanced at Fred.

"No use," he said in a low voice. "They 've got us!"

Then he spoke up to them: "What do you want?"

At that they all gritted their teeth and snarled like wolves again, aspirating "*Sacré!*" away down in their throats. This they did to scare us, I suppose, — to get us thoroughly afraid of them.

THE DOOR WAS KICKED OPEN WITH LOUD AND FIERCE SHOUTS.

At that, Scott began to beg. I do not mean that he got down on his knees; but he said, "Come, now, don't kill us; don't shoot us. We'll do whatever you say."

But the rest of us said nothing.

"Don't talk," said Fred. "Don't say a word to 'em!"

He was right. That was the best way to do,—say nothing. They had no pity nor mercy about them. Begging and pleading would have been just thrown away. They did not, as it appeared, quite dare to kill all four of us; but it wasn't mercy. They were afraid to do it; and they would have killed us all the quicker for our begging. That is the way with such wretches. It always makes them worse to plead with them. The best way is to say not a word. Let them do what they dare; for they will do that, anyway.

"Naw yer coom out aw thart. *Sacré! Sacré!*" they began to say, after they had gritted and snarled at us what they thought proper.

"Coom out aw thart, yer ——! and leave yar guerns, yer ——!"

Fred got right up as soon as they said this, and walked straight out between them, looking them full in the face. Farr followed, and I came next. But Scott hesitated and rather cringingly shied out past them. Seeing his fear, they gritted their teeth at him; and two of them kicked him brutally. If he had held his head up and looked them in the eye like a man, they would not have touched him. Ruffians of this sort are like curs. The only safety from them lies in not fearing them.

They had a large gaunt bull-dog, brindled, with a bobtail. Spot had run out, and stood cowering at a little distance.

"S-t tak 'im!" one of them called out. "S-t tak 'im, Rog!"

Spot cut away for dear life, with Rog, or Rogue, whichever it was, after him. That was the last we saw of either of them.

As soon as we were out in front of the shed, Fred turned, facing them. They pointed their guns at us, three of them,— old army muskets.  I did not know but that they would shoot us down there in our tracks.

"Gav us yer mowny!" they ordered.

"Let them have it," Fred said.

We handed out what scrip we had, — a little rising two dollars.

Evidently they were disappointed in the amount.  They swore again and " *Sacred*" ferociously.

" Tak arf yer coarts," the leader ordered us.

We took them off and gave them up.

" Tak arf yer warst-cuts," was the next requisition.

We unbuttoned our vests, Fred setting the example, and gave them up also.

Then one of them, — a red-eyed, wicked-looking villain, — stepped up, and thrusting his dirty paw into our trowsers' pockets, took out our pocket-knives and whatever other things we had, —combs, pencils, buttons, etc.  And they even made Scott take off his woollen shirt, leaving him in nothing but his under-shirt and pants.  I expected they would strip the rest of us in a similar way, but they did not. Scott's shirt was a rather better one than the rest of us had on. Perhaps they thought our shirts were not worth stealing.

While they were plundering us, I observed them attentively, rather from a sort of fascination than otherwise.  They seemed like men in process of turning to beasts.  There was a restive truculence in their glances, and an air of sullen ferocity in all their movements, such as one sees in wild animals of the fiercer species.  We had no doubt that they were the outlaws, living in the wilderness, of whom we had heard.

" Whuere are yer trarps ? " one of them demanded.

" There are some up at the falls," said Fred.  " There are some in Indian Cove, and some others down at the dam."

" An yar tell us troo ? " cried another.

" Yes ; I have told you true," Fred said.

One of them, in particular, struck me as having the strangest countenance I ever saw. He was forty years old, perhaps, though it was hard guessing his age. His beard was matted, and partially clotted with grease; and his face so flabby that his mouth looked like a mere crease betwixt his lips.

The one that seemed to be captain or leader of the party had very keen black eyes, — eyes that may have been clear and intelligent in boyhood, but which were now hopelessly hardened and sinister. His face was deeply pitted, and had other marks of a wild and lawless life. On every one of their visages there was set the seal of physical and moral depravity.

They had espied the mink and marten skins hanging over our bunk. That seemed to please them somewhat. No doubt they had means of disposing of fur.

This all occupied but a very few minutes. As soon as they had robbed us, — to our shirts and pants, — the leader pointed to the bateau.

" Be gittin' inter thart ! " he sang out to us.

We started obediently. While we were going to it, one of them fired off a gun behind us. I heard the shot whistle past our heads; still, I am inclined to think it was done merely to scare us.

We got into the boat. I thought they were going to let us go off in it; but they came behind us with their guns and got into it with us.

" I guess they are going to take us down the lake," Farr whispered, as we huddled together in the bow.

He was wrong. They merely paddled across to the opposite bank. We did not know what they intended to do, and so sat still after the boat touched.

" Out ! yar ——— ! " they shouted.

We got out.

They got out after us and covered us with their guns.

We trembled then.

"Now, thin!" yelled the one that led, gritting his teeth till he fairly foamed at his mouth; "be arf wit ye! yar——! Stiver! Nevair coom bark! Mog!"

There being no help for it, we *mogged* — as fast as we could, taking a course that would take us out to our "saple" line. They followed on after us for half a mile or upwards to see that we really went off; and they fired at us once at a distance, to let us know what we might expect if we came back; I, for one, had no idea of going back.

We followed down the "saple" line. As soon as we found that the robbers had gone back and left us, we ran for a mile, at least. Not much was said; they had not left us much to talk about. We were robbed of everything and driven out. For my own part, I felt for several hours completely cowed, — whipped. There we were, forty miles from settlement, without arms; we had not even a jack-knife.

It was not till we had crossed Moose Brook, that even a word was exchanged. There Farr said, "Where are you going, Fred?"

"Down to the gorge camp," was the answer.

"What good will that do?" Scott demanded querulously.

"What good!" exclaimed Fred. "Why, I rather guess we shall want to be getting outside of some of that sprung pork by the time we get down there. I, for one, have n't been to breakfast yet."

We had none of us thought of breakfast.

On the ridge, near the lower end of the lake, we found a marten in one of the "dead-falls." What a mockery it seemed to our trapping scheme! Fred took it out, however, and carried it along.

We crossed the dam, and got to the camp at a little before eight o'clock.

How different our feelings now from what they had been when we came here three weeks before. However, we set at work to get breakfast from supplies there. We fried some meat, boiled some beans, and cooked *water* biscuits. The beans we ate with salt; the biscuits we dipped in the pork fat. By heating it very hot, we fancied we had taken the "sprung" out of it. It was the best we had; and persons must eat, whatever comes.

But we did not dare to stay long at the camp. Our captors might find us there. We were utterly defenceless. We took a frying-pan, a tin-dipper, two case-knives, two tin-plates, and the large "pot" that went with the stove. This latter utensil we packed full of pork. There was also a two-gallon coffee-pot, — an old affair. This we filled with flour; and as there was nothing else in our pants' pockets, we filled those with beans and tea. We argued that our case was one of absolute necessity, and so it was.

There was an old axe at this camp. Fred took that; also an old butcher-knife, which he stuck in his waistband. Farr took a bunch of matches from the quarter gross put away in the cuddy.

Thus equipped, we started down the "carry," toward the forks and toward home.

# CHAPTER XX.

IF ever the world looked dark to four youngsters, it did to us. At first we had been too glad to get away from the "Cannucks" (as Fred called them) to think much about the future. But now that we were fairly out of their clutches, and started for the settlements, the full bitterness of our situation began to break upon us. We had staked a great deal, for us, on this expedition; and to be defeated in this humiliating way was unbearable.

We reproached ourselves for not keeping guard continually. Then we should not have been surprised, and, in a word, *ruined*.

We thought now of the figure we should cut returning home in our shirts and pants, without our guns; and of the chapfallen story we should have to tell; and how the folks who predicted our failure at the outset would inwardly chuckle while they pretended to pity us. Pity us they might; but there would be their inevitable " I told you so."

The story would get out; and then how inquisitive people would be, and how they would laugh over it, and say we had better have stayed at home.

And then where were our funds to go to the Academy the next spring to come from? We talked, or rather croaked, these dismal views to each other as we plodded down the carry, till our hearts grew hard and wicked in our jacketless bosoms; till we grew quite desperate and reckless; and till at last Fred threw down the old pot of pork and vowed he would not go home another step!

"What's the use to go home!" he exclaimed hotly. "I vow on my head, I had as lief be shot as go home in this way!"

Rash words. But I have no doubt he felt them, for the moment at least. Farr and I felt much in the same way, although we neither of us had the grit to say it outright.

"But what *shall* we do?" Scott asked dubiously.

"I don't know," said Fred, candidly. "But I won't go home so! May I die on the road if I do!"

He was in dead earnest.

We sat down on a windfall and looked at each other. A crisis had come in our affairs. This outrage had goaded us to desperation. I suppose that many of the reckless exploits and desperate deeds which astonish the world are done under similar stress of ill-luck and passion. When a fellow is driven clean to the wall, then look out for him — if he has spirit; for if he has, he will never go down without one grand effort to retrieve himself. Desperate men hit hard.

Off to the right of the carry path (going down) there is a little pond, named by some wandering hunter "Sunday Pond." We had espied it the day we carried our bateau up to the lake. It is a pretty little expanse almost circular in shape and perhaps half a mile in diameter, set in a natural basin, and surrounded by the thick spruce forest.

"Let's go out to the pond and look about, and get breath," Fred at last said.

So, departing from our line of retreat, we went down through the woods to the pond shore. Here we sat down on an old drift-log near the water's edge, and looked at each other again, a pretty long spell.

"What's the use to stay in this savage region?" was about all Scott had to say.

And "I won't go home" was all we could get out of Fred. But this much was decisive.

Farr and I said nothing: we could think of nothing to say, to the point; and at such times persons are not apt to talk to no purpose. We sat there and brooded for two hours, certainly.

"Well, if we 're going to stay here, let 's make us a camp some-where," Farr at length broke out.

The rest of us agreed to that.

Fred then led off, following the shore of the pond round to the southwest side, where there was a little brook leading out of it down to the Little Magalloway, of which the pond is tributary. Crossing this, we came to a rick of great rocks on the hill-side above it.

"Might make us a den among these," Farr suggested.

Without waste of words, Fred set down the pot of pork and began to cut poles. These we laid across the tops of three of the large rocks that lay about and near to each other, and then thatched them over with boughs of spruce and fir. The little space enclosed by the rocks was partially filled with dry leaves, twigs, and the fallen foliage of the spruces. This, with sprigs of fir, offered a decent bed. Scott shivered with cold, in his undershirt. Fred peeled off, as well as could be done at this season of the year, a broad slab of bark from a large canoe-birch, out of which we contrived a sort of jacket for our scantily clad comrade.

As for the rest of us, we did not feel uncomfortably cold in our woollen shirts while at work. It was only on sitting down that we shivered.

The most of that afternoon was spent in getting up a good meal out of such as we had. We could at least afford a generous fire; our only anxiety on this score being lest the Cannucks should see the smoke. But as the pond was not in sight from the lake or its immediate shores, we had no great fear of it.

We were, as we reckoned it, twelve miles from the Cleaveland camp.

For coverlets that night we had nothing but boughs and birch-

SCOTT'S BIRCH-BARK JACKET.

bark; but we built a great fire before the rocks, and lay close to each other, in order to lose no warmth. Despite our nestling, we got pretty cold toward morning.

Fred got up before light and rebuilt the fire.

Just at sunrise there came on another violent snow-squall. The woods sighed and roared. It darkened; and the snowflakes fell thickly. It made us shudder. Winter was evidently at no great distance; and what, alas! was our situation?

At breakfast, which we at length got, Fred said, " They surprised us; what's the reason we can't surprise them?"

"With an old axe and a butcher-knife!" Scott exclaimed derisively.

Fred went on to explain that they would not always be at the camp, — all of them, at least.

"But how do you know they are there, or stayed there an hour?" said I.

"Oh, they'll stay there and trap there awhile," said Fred. " I know they will. That's why they drove us off, — they wanted our chance. But they will be on their guard for a day or two," he added, after a long pause.

During the forenoon, Farr made the remark that if we were going to stay there we might as well go to digging gum as to do nothing.

That seemed sensible. Hope revived a little. Possibly we might make a trifle yet. All about us there was a heavy spruce growth, and on many of the trunks we had noticed gum, — large balls of it.

" But what are we to dig it with?" Scott questioned.

" Here's the axe," said Farr.

" And the butcher-knife," said Fred.

" That will be for two only," objected Scott. (He was homesick enough those days; he wanted to start for home.)

" There are the case-knives," I said.

But they were too limber.

That fault was in part remedied by breaking them off midway the blade.

To hold the gum after it was dug, we provided ourselves with dishes, or trays, made of birch-bark, fastened together at the corners with wooden pins.

This finding something to do was a godsend to us. Work takes up a fellow's mind. We grew quite cheerful going from tree to tree to dig the gum. It is rather pretty work, too, — light and cheery. There is a pleasure in finding rare "good trees" and big lumps. Some trees would be quite crusted with it on one side from the ground upward for twenty or thirty feet. But we could not reach higher than six or seven feet. Sometimes gumming parties bind a chisel to a long pole. There is also manufactured what is called a *gummer*, — an instrument made on purpose for the business.

We had to use such instruments as we had in hand. Nevertheless, in three or four hours we dug not less than six quarts of clear gum: about four pounds of it, we judged; and we reckoned it worth not less than two dollars.

When a party has had a long run of misfortune, even little encouragements cheer them.

"We will take home what clear gum we can carry," Farr said; "and we can carry a hundred-weight between us. That will be fifty dollars, certain."

# CHAPTER XXI.

## HARD TIMES.

THAT night it came in cloudy, with the weather cold and piercing. We had bad luck with our fire. It burned but poorly. There are some nights that a camp-fire will not burn even if the wood be good. It kept deadening down, and smouldered.

Something was round the camp, too, — some creature. Perhaps it had followed us in from gumming, though we did not hear it till as late as eight o'clock in the evening. If we had only had a gun we would have made it scamper! Fred did not care for it; he lay down and went to sleep. But it disturbed me thoroughly; I could not go to sleep. No more could Scott; and I think Farr did not rest any too well. I noticed he kept one hand on the butcher-knife. We could hear twigs break, off a little way. I fancied I could see its eyes. Repeatedly I heard its step. It kept prowling about till near morning. We had little idea what it was; the night was too dark to discern anything off from the fire.

Toward morning I fell into a sound nap.

When I woke, Farr and Scott were snoring well; but Fred was gone. He did not come back till near nine o'clock. We guessed, however, that he had gone off to reconnoitre, and so got breakfast ready and waited: that is to say, we waited five or ten minutes, then ate our share of it and kept the rest warm for him.

He came in warm and tired.

"Wherever have you been?" we asked.

He had been up as far as Indian Point, — seven miles, at least. He had seen nothing of the Cannucks; but there was a smoke visible over the woods in the direction of the old camp; and he had no doubt that they were there yet.

We went out to dig gum again; and that day we dug what we called five pounds. It gave us some idea of the vast quantities in these woods. There were, we perceived, tons of it. The supply was inexhaustible, so far as we were concerned.

That day Fred killed a partridge with a stone. We had it for supper. The reader may rest assured that we did not throw away any part of that bird. There was no Spot to eat the wings and legs raw. Poor Spot! We supposed that the big brindled dog — Rogue — had eaten him up.

That night it snowed an inch or two.

Fred went off early again to reconnoitre the Cannucks. On coming back he told us that he had been to the high land on the west side of the lake, to the mouth of Bosebuck; and he had heard the report of a gun up near the head of the lake.

"They are trapping up there, full blast," said he. " The wretches! Is n't it awful aggravating? *Our* traps, *our* grub, *our* guns, and *our* camp!"

It was too aggravating to dwell on! It was enough to turn a fellow's blood to gall!

We gummed five or six pounds that day.

Farr killed a leveret (young hare) with a pole. We had rabbit for supper.

"Rather weak stuff," so Scott said; and it was so. But it was better than sprung pork, — for a change, at least.

That night it was windy. We slept very cold.

Scott had now begun to sneeze about half the time. He nearly sneezed himself out of his birch-bark jacket. He had cold-sores, and sore eyes, beside.

FARR KILLED A YOUNG HARE.

Poor wretch! we pitied him. That was all we could do, — except to make him white-birch jackets; and that was no small job, for he shook them to pieces sneezing.

Those were tough times. I don't see how we lived. But we were too outrageously angry to die. Most of all things, we wanted to get square with those beastly Cannucks.

# CHAPTER XXII.

### OUR TURN NEXT!

THE morning after, Fred and I went up to the lake together to see whether any of our enemies were abroad. From our camp, or rather den, among the rocks at Sunday Pond, up to the lake, it was about three miles, — perhaps three and a half. We came out on the shore at the foot of Bose-buck Cove, and stood gazing off up the lake toward the islands, distant nearly five miles.

Presently, as we looked, I saw a speck moving across the open stretch, between two of the islands. Fred saw it at the same moment.

"What's that?" he said. "Is n't that a boat?"

It seemed likely.

"Yes, sir: that's our old bateau, sure's you're born, Frank!" Fred exclaimed, a moment later. "Coming down the lake, too."

We hastily retreated out of sight among the alders, and then watched the boat eagerly, anxiously.

It came on pretty fast. In half an hour it was in plain sight; and not long after we made out four persons in it.

"They are going down to the dam!" exclaimed Fred. "Now's our time!"

"But they 've left a man at the camp," I objected.

"Yes; but he may not be on his guard," said Fred. "Now's our time to strike. He may step out a moment, and if he does, why, we 'll step in. Stay here and watch the boat. I 'll run for the other boys."

He was off like a shot.

It seemed a desperate enterprise; but we were in desperate straits, ready to run risks.

The bateau crawled down the lake, and at length entered the outlet and disappeared.

How long they would stay down at the dam and the camp there was a mere matter of conjecture.

Fred must have run all the way down to the pond; for in less than an hour they all three came panting through the woods: Farr greatly excited and half-crazy, and Scott looking pale but determined. Once started on such an errand he was not the boy to show the white feather.

Fred had the axe and butcher-knife. He cut down a hornbeam sapling, and armed the rest of us each with a formidable club. We then went up the slope to the height of land. There we struck our old "saple" line on the west side of the lake. This we followed up the west shore.

Fred went ahead, half the time at a dog-trot. The rest of us with our clubs kept up as best we could. Where we could see out through the woods on to the lake, we stopped to take a look. Each time it rejoiced our hearts to see that the bateau had not yet come out in sight at the foot of the lake. Then on we would go again.

I do not think we were much over an hour going up.

On getting within a half mile of the camp, however, we advanced very cautiously; and when within fifty rods we spoke only in whispers, and dared not let so much as a twig break under our feet.

At length from among a clump of alders we caught sight of it, — the back side of it. A smoke was rising lazily. We could even smell the burning wood. All was quiet; nobody in sight.

"He's inside making something, or perhaps taking a snooze," Farr suggested.

We stood watching for ten or fifteen minutes. We knew that time was precious, too. Even now the bateau might be on its way up the lake!

"I'm going to see who's there, anyhow," Fred whispered.

He crept forward, axe in hand. Moving to the right, so as to bring the main ox-camp between him and the grain-shed, he went quickly up to within a dozen yards of it. Then, after listening a moment, he stole forward to peep through the cracks in the side of it. But before he was near enough for this a dog barked out on a sudden. Instantly Fred dropped behind a stump. Our hearts beat loudly. We expected to see a Cannuck rush out, gun in hand.

But nothing stirred, though the dog continued barking boisterously from within the shed. We saw Fred creep forward. He peeped through the cracks, then, as if reassured, crawled around the end to look at the front side. Then he jumped to his feet and called "Come on!" to us. "There's nobody here."

We ran out to the shed.

"There's not a soul here," Fred said, as we came up. "He's off somewhere. Left the dog shut in to watch. But he'll soon be back if he hears the barking. We'll put an end to it. Be ready with your clubs." Fred unbuttoned the door. It swung partly open. Out leaped Rogue, all bristle and growl. Farr struck him across the head with his club, on the instant. The blow stunned him. Fred at once despatched the cur with the axe.

"One the less of them," said Farr.

"Be on the lookout," Fred advised. "You, Scott, and Farr."

He and I went into the shed.

"Skins are gone!" Fred exclaimed at first glance. "They've either hidden them or sent them off."

I was looking for the guns. There were four, standing up in one corner, all loaded: two of their old muskets, one of our double-barrelled guns (Farr's), and Fred's single-barrel. The little rifle and our other double-barrel were gone.

OUT LEAPED ROGUE, ALL BRISTLE AND GROWL.

"Got them with them in the bateau," said Farr.

The ammunition — a part of it — lay on the little shelf where we had kept it. We at once drew the charges and reloaded the guns.

Farr ran into the ox-camp.

"There are ten musk-rat skins and one of the mink-skins gone," he reported.

"Then I'll tell you what's up!" Fred exclaimed. "They've sent a man off — out into Canada somewhere — after rum, with those skins and the scrip they got from us. That's what's the matter!"

We could find nothing of our coats, or waistcoats either, and thought it quite likely that they had sent these off too.

The hide of some creature had been nailed up to the side of the ox-camp. meat side out. We pulled it down. It was *the skin of poor Spot!*

"There's all there is left of your dog, Farr," said Fred.

The sight of that skin made Charles Henry's eyes snap.

"Poor Spot!" was all we could say; and there lay Rogue, too, dead as a hammer. Truly this had been a hard week for dogs.

"But don't stand fooling there!" Fred exclaimed. "We've not a moment to lose. The bateau will soon be back, *and then what?*"

"We won't let them land," said Farr. "We will stand with our guns cocked and pointed, and drive them off."

"And lose the bateau and what there is in it!" cried Fred. "That won't do! We must work shrewder than that. I'll tell you," said he, after a little thought. "Let's get inside the shed, shut the door, and lie quiet till they land. Then we will stop 'em short when they are coming up to the camp from the boat."

"What! shoot them?" I exclaimed.

"No; if we work it right there'll be no need of that. They are a set of sneaks. They won't fight if they see we have the advantage. We'll have our guns all ready, cocked, and aimed at their heads before they see us. I 'll do the talking. Don't shoot, any of you, unless I give the word. We won't hurt them unless we 're obliged to. But we 'll have our things back, anyhow. They don't deserve to live, the scoundrels! But we won't shed their dirty blood. We 'll save 'em for the gallows. Now, fellows, keep cool. Don't get scared. Keep cool! That's half the battle. If we 've got any pluck about us, we must show it now. Now's the time to show what stuff we 're made of."

Instead of the shed, we concluded to lie in ambush in the ox-camp. The door-way of the latter was larger, and we could step out quicker.

The carcass of old Rogue we threw inside the shed, and shut the door, just as they had left it. We even nailed Spot's skin to the side of the ox-camp again.

It was now a little past noon. We kept out of sight in the camp and waited.

An hour passed. It was this having to wait that tried our courage most of all. As long as we could put things through with a rush, we felt pretty brave. We had no thoughts of backing out, however; but the delay made us nervous.

Finally, about two o'clock, we heard the sound of paddles coming up the stream, and soon rough voices. Our hearts jumped, — at least my own did. I *felt* pale, and I noticed the other boys *looked* so. We shut our teeth hard and braced ourselves.

Nearer came the sounds. Each fresh noise sent a thrill through me. Only Fred stood where he could peep out.

The boat came slowly up to the landing-place. They were talking in French, — Canadian French. Their voices were coarse. We knew enough of their talk to perceive that their words were nearly all oaths. The sound of paddles stopped. I heard them unshipping their oars.

" Be ready," Fred whispered.

They were getting out.

Still Fred stood motionless.

" They 've stolen a barrel of that pork down at the other camp," he whispered, at length.  " They 're unloading it.  Now they 've begun to roll it up toward the camp.  They 've left their guns in the boat.  Be ready ! "

I could hear the heavy barrel crunching on the stones and chips ; could hear even their breathings as they rolled it along, with now and then an ejaculated French word or curse.

" *Now !* " Fred whispered, and stepped noiselessly out.  We followed him.

They were not a dozen yards off ; but they were bent over and did not see us even then.

" Halt, there ! " Fred shouted.

You ought to have seen them jump!  One of them jumped up a foot from the ground !  We had our guns pointed full in their faces.

" Stand where you are ! " Fred said distinctly.

They stood and stared ; they were astounded.  One of them turned partially, as if to run to the bateau.

" Stop ! " Fred shouted.  " If you stir, I 'll shoot you dead ! " taking aim at him.

He stopped.

" It 's our turn now," said Fred.  " You had your turn.  But now we 've got you.  If you offer the least resistance, we will kill you on the spot !  We 'll shoot you down like dogs ! "  They stared at the muzzles of the guns stupidly.

" Turn that barrel up on end ! " ordered Fred, advancing with his double-barrelled gun pointed directly among them.  Two of them stooped and turned it up.

" Now put our knives and whatever you stole from us on it," Fred ordered.

They hesitated alarmedly ; they did not understand.

"*Couteau-canif!*" shouted Fred, slapping his pocket and pointing to the head of the barrel.

Then they knew what was wanted, and fumbled the knives and trinkets out one by one, the most of them, and laid them down as directed.

"Now the 'mowney' you stole from us!" Fred sang out.

They looked scared, shook their heads. "No got," they said. "No got. Gorne," pointing off up the river.

"Hand it out!" Fred yelled at them.

"No got! no got! gorne!" they protested. "Peter gorne!"

We saw that the one who acted as their leader when they robbed us was really gone. He was probably the Peter referred to.

"Where are our 'coarts' and 'warst-cuts'?" Fred demanded.

"Gorne! gorne!" they chorused.

At that Fred pretended to be terribly enraged. He took aim at them; so did we all.

They cowered, but kept saying, "Gorne! gorne!"

We had little doubt of it.

"Pull off those boots!" thundered Fred, pointing to Scott's rubber boots, which one of them had on.

The villain obeyed with great promptness, and set them together as far from him as he could well reach.

"Take off your 'coarts,'" said Fred.

They took them off.

"Take off your 'warst-cuts.'"

They began to obey, but one of them grumbled audibly.

"Not a *yip* out of you!" Fred shouted.

The rest of us covered him with our guns. The vest came off quickly, and was laid with the others.

"I've a great mind to strip them stark naked," Fred muttered.

"I guess I would n't," said Scott. "It is n't best to behave worse than they did. But I should like my shirt back."

"Off with that shirt!" exclaimed Fred, pointing his gun at one of the best-looking of their shirts, worn by the man with the crease mouth.

He pulled it off. It left him bare to his dirty hairy skin.

"Have we served them bad enough?" Fred now questioned.

I thought so, for one.

"I guess they will do," Farr said.

"All right," said Fred. "Now take aim at them, sharp."

We aimed as if about to shoot them down. I rather think they expected it. No doubt they were well aware that they deserved it.

Fred pointed off up the river.

"Stiver!" he shouted. "Mog! you won't find us napping again!"

They started hesitatingly, as if half-afraid to move.

"Mog!" Fred reiterated.

They quickened their steps, with eyes over their shoulders.

"Run!" we all yelled after them.

Then they ran — for life, through the brush along the river. No doubt they expected we would fire after them.

We kept shouting, then ran on after them half-way up to Little Boy's Falls. But we soon lost sight of them; for they scudded away like foxes.

# CHAPTER XXIII.

### THE LOG CAMP ON THE KNOLL.

THUS ended the affair for that day.

In the bateau we found the other double-barrelled gun and the other of their old muskets; but the little rifle was gone. We concluded that Peter had taken that too. Fred's jack-knife was not in the pile on the barrel-head. One of our combs, too, was missing, as also several other trinkets.

Their old dirty waistcoats we had no disposition to put on. But the shirt Scott put in soak that night, and the next day dried it and clothed himself in it, — not without certain inward misgivings and a great deal of repugnance.

One of the coats was an army dress-coat, a good deal worn and soiled. Another was an army overcoat with the skirts cut off. The two others were frocks made of coon-skins, the hair turned in. The reader can guess how they looked!

We first shook them, then we smoked them over the fire, then hung them in the wind. But there was a certain odor about them that could not be shaken out. As it grew colder, however, we were glad to put them on. The coon-skins especially were remarkably warm garments.

We skinned Rogue; and after the hide had dried Fred made Scott a waistcoat out of it; and on the same pattern Farr made one for himself out of Spot's skin.

We found in the shed two blankets, which we were very sure were two of the four stolen from us when the old camp was burned. We had no doubt that it was the same party.

There was also a large powder-horn full of shot, and a tin canteen nearly full of Hazard powder.   Both of these we found hidden amid the boughs of the bunk.   There was an old Colt's revolver lying with them, loaded with buck-shot, and a rusty dirk-knife.

We did good sentinel-duty that night; indeed, none of us slept much.   The excitement of the day had keyed us up too high.

We watched alternately, with guns ready for instant use.   There was a moon.

The situation of the old shed, in connection with the ox-camp, was unfavorable for defence.   About twenty rods to the north of it a high knoll, covered with dry spruce-tops, where the trees had been cut, commanded it in most approved military fashion ; and there were thickets on the west and south sides, from any of which a concealed Cannuck might fire upon us.   We had little doubt that they would come back and watch for an opportunity to surprise us.

The following morning we held a serious council.

" Will it not be better to pack up, find what of our traps we can, and go off, — down to Metallic Pond, say, — and leave them ' alone in their glory ' ? " Scott questioned.   " Then we shall be sure of no more trouble from them."

For my own part, I was much of Scott's mind in this.

" When that blear-eyed, pit-faced captain of theirs gets back with the rum, there 'll be a great to-do about this," Scott went on.   " They 'll come round here again, trying to get revenge ; and we shall have a fight with them, likely as not."

But Fred would not hear a word to leaving on this account.

" I 'll not be driven out by any such set of ruffians," he declared. " They 've no business here whatever.   They are a lot of ' deserters ' and ' bounty-jumpers ' from the army, — now turned into robbers and perhaps murderers.   I 'll not run for any such trash !   They 've no business whatever on the soil of this State.   I won't budge for them an inch.   If I see one of them hanging round here again, it will be the worse for him. And as for their firing at us, they will find that we can fire back. We 've got the upper hands of them now, and I for one mean to keep the upper hand."

At such talk as this we all began to wax warlike again. We had not run from them yet, and did not mean to do so. Let them come if they wanted to. They would find a hot reception. They would not find us all asleep again with the door unfastened: so we talked.

Then it was debated how we should fortify our camp, to prevent a surprise, evenings and nights.

" Let 's tear down the old ox-camp and build a strong palisade round our shed here," Scott proposed.

But the rest of us did not like the way the knoll overlooked the shed. We went up on the knoll to look about, taking our guns, of course, and keeping a careful eye about us.

This knoll was some twenty or thirty feet higher than the ox-camp. On the side next the river it fell off very steep to the water. On the west and north sides the declivity was not so great. On the lower side, next the camp, it was rather steep. The best of the spruces had been cut off. But there were scattering trees all about.

From the top of the knoll it was what Fred called " all clear shooting " for fifteen or twenty rods on all sides.

" Why not build a camp up here? " Farr said.

After some talk we concluded we could not do better. Axes were brought up, — those put away in the old grain-box. We set to work chopping, all four of us, in good earnest. The spruces were felled, and cut up into logs thirteen feet long (about that).

I remember that we cut six logs apiece, — twenty-four in all. With these we next proceeded to build the walls of a shed. On three sides we built up with the logs, notching and locking the ends together as is done in building a log camp, or house of any sort. But we left the front side open, and to secure the ends of the end logs, where, as in a full-sided camp, the front-side logs should have locked across

THERE WAS A MOON.

them, we drove down stout stakes on both sides and bound them together with strong withs. The heaviest logs we placed at the bottom, and then rolled the lighter ones up into their places on skids.

These walls were about six feet high; hardly that, though, I think, on reflection.

The roof we made of ash poles, over which we laid splits from the old shed.

On the open front side we hung up the tent, which we found in the shed as we left it, with the exception of a square bit cut out for a patch for some of their clothes. It furnished us with a very good door or curtain to our hut.

The building of this hut occupied all the forenoon; we worked hard, too. But we had a still harder task planned for afternoon. For we had no thought of trusting ourselves in the shed with no other protection.

" We must have a wall round it," Fred declared.

But as stones were scarce, and the building of a stone wall would have been a great task, we decided to make a stockade of logs. And that was no small job.

During all the afternoon, allowing ourselves only an hour for dinner, we toiled till the sun set, and raised a huge fence nine feet high on all sides of the hut. This fence was of logs laid upon each other, much like ordinary log fences, only snug together, leaving but few cracks.

It was about thirty-six feet square on the outside, and consequently left a walk about ten feet wide around the hut inside the fence. The hut was our *castle*, and the fence was our castle-wall.

The only door-way through the fence was a hole about three feet square. Through this we crept. For a door we brought up the door from the grain-shed, and set it sidewise betwixt stakes on the inside in such a way that no one could open it from the outside. Whichever of us happened to be on guard had to open it for the rest of us when we returned from our trips to visit traps, or otherwise.

Inside the fence we had a platform of logs built up, where the guard could stand and look off over the top of the fence.

That was a hard afternoon's work. Just at dusk we carried up the old stove and set it up inside the stockade.

The Cannucks had made a great hole in our potatoes. Evidently they had found them very palatable; and they had eaten up nearly the whole of our butter. This was very vexatious.

"The scamps!" Fred would ejaculate. "I wish we had stripped them to their skins and slit their noses for 'em!"

It was dark before we had got fairly moved into our new quarters. But once in there, within our nine-foot fence, with the "sheep-hole" (as Farr called the door) stopped up, we felt much more secure.

"They would have hard work to get over *that* before we could pop them!" Fred said.

We took care to have our guns loaded and at hand.

I have often thought since that we were rather bloodily-minded in those days. Yet what else could we do? If we stayed we must defend ourselves; and Fred was determined to stay. He certainly had a right to stay, though I suppose a genuine peace-maker would have thought it better to go away at once. But there must be some fighting in the world, else the peace-makers themselves would soon have a hard time of it.

# CHAPTER XXIV.

FOR the sake of regularity and convenience, we divided the night into four watches : the first from eight, evening, till half-past ten ; the second from half-past ten till one, morning ; the third from one till half-past three ; the fourth from that time till six, the hour for rising. And here Scott's old watch — which he carried without a guard in a little inside pocket within the waistband of his pants, and which escaped the general robbery by the Cannucks — did us good service.

It had a curious semblance of military life, — our hours of guard-duty by night, and the constant vigilance with which we watched days. I well remember that first night in the new camp. I had the watch from one till half-past three. It was chilly. The stars shone brightly. There were occasional windy gusts, to which the vast sombre forest rustled and sighed. The falls roared at a distance ; and nearer, at the foot of the knoll, I could hear the fret of the black current on the banks, and catch the silvery reflection of stars. A saw-whet owl was practising at a distance. Once a bear called out in lonely plaint. A hooting owl answered. But the hours were hours of silence and desolation, for the most part.

And thus it has been here, I reflected, through all the ages since time began. No wonder that wildness and loneliness have become stamped ineffably as it were on these wilderness regions.

The next morning Farr was detailed to do guard-duty at camp for the day. Fred, Scott, and I set off to make the round of the "saple" line, and look to our traps at the lower end of the lake. We went armed each with a gun; and Fred took the old revolver which Farr had loaded with the bullets run for the broken carbine.

On the east side of the lake we found two martens dead in the traps. We concluded that the Cannucks had not hit upon the "saple" traps. But they had found our traps at the dam, and moved them into different places: three were found; the others were re-moved to some other locality, we presumed.

Down at the rapids we found a mink in a trap, dead also. It had probably been caught four or five days previously. These traps were all as we had left them.

In the marten traps on the west shore of the lake there was one marten, just caught evidently, for he was still warm, though the heavy weight had broken his back.

We hurried a good deal, and made this entire round in a little more than five hours.

Farr reported all quiet, with no signs of Cannucks.

Dinner was got and eaten. Then we went down the stream in the bateau to look to the musk-rat traps in Indian Cove. The Cannucks had been here. The traps had been changed about, but we found all save four. There were five musk-rats caught.

This trip took us about two hours, and we still had time to go up to Little Boy's Falls. Of the traps we had set here, the Canadians had removed all but two. In one of these there had been a mink, but he had footed himself and gone.

That was a hard day's work. We reckoned the entire profit from the fur at thirteen dollars,—three dollars and a quarter apiece.

That night Fred had the second watch, and at about twelve he waked us.

"Just come out here a minute," he said.

We roused up and went out. Fred was standing on the log plat-form; and we got up beside him.

" Hark ! " he said.

We listened. Some moments passed. Then, distinct on the cold air, there came a singularly prolonged and piercing cry from seemingly a long way off.

" I 've heard that more than a dozen times," said Fred.

" Any idea what it is ? " Farr asked him.

" No ; never heard anything like it before in my life."

It was repeated again and again, at intervals of five or ten minutes.

" I don't believe that it is an animal," Farr said.

" Is n't it the Cannucks trying to frighten us ? " Scott said.

That question made us laugh. It was a rather improbable supposition.

We went back to our sleep.

Fred said next day that the sound had continued for an hour or over after we had gone to sleep.

And the next night Farr waked us at a few minutes after two to hear the same cries again. They seemed even more distinct this time. But we could gain no idea as to what produced them.

The second night after, Scott told us that at a quarter before five o'clock he had heard it twice, but very faint and far off. I do not think that even the second time we heard it, it was within three miles of the camp.

" Ah, I tell you, fellows, there are things in these woods that folks do not know of," Fred would say occasionally. This was a pet idea of his ; and, indeed, we never did know what made that noise ; we could not even guess with any certainty.

The fourth night after moving up to our fortified camp it was very dark and cloudy; and at a few minutes after eight it came on to snow, — a driving storm. I had the first watch, but was glad to get down from the post of duty and take refuge inside the shed.

" I guess the Cannucks won't stir out to-night," Fred said.

It was agreed to watch inside our camp-curtain. But at about half-past one there was a noise outside, on the log-fence, as of some one trying to climb it. Farr was on guard. He instantly cocked his gun, listened an instant, then peeped out very cautiously; for he knew that if there were enemies inside the fence, they would fire into the camp at the slightest indication of our wakefulness.

The storm was driving so thickly, and the darkness was so great, that he could see nothing. But he stood ready for instant defence for fifteen or twenty minutes; then he quietly waked the rest of us, and in whispers informed us of what he suspected. We all took our guns and listened a long while. At length Fred crept out under the curtain with his revolver in one hand and the butcher-knife betwixt his teeth !

He was out ten minutes or more, and on coming in, reported that he could find nothing either within or without the fence. But Farr was positive that he had heard a considerable noise. Afterward we thought that it might have been a wild-cat, or a bear that had smelled our meat.

But the alarm had so excited us that we none of us went to sleep again till near five o'clock.

That morning the country presented a wintry appearance. The firs and spruce were laden with the snow, and the ground was ghostly white. The open stream at the foot of the knoll looked like a river of ink in its white banks. It was still snowing.

Getting breakfast that morning was a work of time.

Toward ten o'clock the storm ceased. About four inches had fallen.

"We've got a sweet job before us, to dig out all our traps and set them up again," Fred remarked.

He and I started down the river in the bateau to look to the musk-rat traps, leaving Scott and Farr in camp. We were just emerging into the lake, when Fred stopped paddling.

" Hold on," said he: " I believe, on my soul, that 's a moose ! "

" Where ? " I exclaimed.

" Right out between these islands ahead; on Indian Point," said Fred. " Don't you see something there ? "

The distance was half a mile or over; but on the snowy shore of the Point, among the bushes near the water's edge, I plainly discerned some large animal moving about.

" That 's a moose, sure as you 're breathing ! " Fred exclaimed excitedly. " Now, how are we going to get him ? Antlers, too! Don't you see them ? A big stag moose ! We must have that old chap. But the minute he sets eyes on us you 'll hear a smashing ! And he will see us up here if we don't look out."

" Can we not surround him ? " said I. " By going down through the woods we could cut him off, so he could not leave the Point without our getting a shot at him."

" Yes ; but he would take to the water," said Fred. " The moment he heard us coming up the Point, behind him, he would splash into the lake and fin it across to the east shore. But I have it ! " he exclaimed. " We will two of us come down in the bateau at the same time; and if he takes to the water, we will overhaul him in the boat."

As quickly, yet with as little noise as possible, we pulled back up to the camp.

Farr and Scott were both excited when they heard our account.

" But who will guard the camp ? " I said.

That was a poser. We all wanted to go after the moose; yet we all agreed that it was not safe for all to leave camp. The Cannucks might come.

" Shall have to draw lots for it," Fred said.

But here Scott did a magnanimous thing.

" I 'll stay," said he. " Go ahead, the rest of you; I 'll keep guard."

Upon that both Farr and myself were seized with a fit of generosity. We offered to stay in his place.

"No," said Scott; "I 'll stay this time."

"Come on, then," Fred exclaimed.  "Load up for moose !"

Both of the double-barrelled guns and two of the old muskets were charged with bullets.

It was agreed for one of us to run down through the woods on the west side of the lake to Indian Point and cut off the moose, to prevent his leaving the Point, while the other two went in the bateau, as Fred had planned.

Farr volunteered to run down through the woods, and set off at a trot with one of the double-barrels.

Fred and I rowed back down the stream as fast as we could.

As Indian Point projects for a third of a mile or upwards into the lake, we had not much fear of the moose getting back off of it, especially as he appeared, when we saw him, to be leisurely feeding.

On coming out on the lake, Fred and I kept on the lee of the second island ; but we pulled out to near the lower end of it, where we could peep through the alder fringe.  From here we at first saw nothing of the moose.

"I 'm afraid he heard us, and is gone," Fred said.  "Their ears are quicker than magic oil !"

We were in an eager suspense, and hung there waiting for Farr to get down.  He had some two miles and a half to go.

Presently we heard a hound, "Ough, ough, ough !" from the woods off beyond the Point.

"A hunting party !" Fred exclaimed, with a look of distress.

But the regular bay soon changed to a "yap."

"That 's no hound," said I.

"That 's Farr barking," cried Fred disgustedly.  "Well, let him bark.  It 's the best thing he can do."

Soon after we heard a gun.

"If the moose is on the Point, he will soon be out in sight," muttered Fred ; and he was correct in his surmise.  Immediately we saw the bushes swaying; and a second afterward the moose sprang through them, and stood in the edge of the water, his great ears held up alertly, and his head turned to glance into the woods behind him. So motionless did he stand there, listening, that I should have taken him for a great black upturned root. Then he ran along the shore, through the bushes and brush, for several rods around the end to the south side. We held our breaths.

" He 's going to cut out past Farr," Fred groaned.

But a moment later we heard more barking; and the moose came tearing back round to the north side again.

The moose had not seen any of us yet; for Farr was not within a hundred rods of him, and the woods were thick. But the old fellow knew that something wrong was going on. We could see his great ears rising at each fresh sound.

Another report came wafted across the lake; and, even before the sound of it had reached us, we saw the moose plunge into the water, and strike off diagonally toward the east shore, — not toward the islands.

" Now go for him!" cried Fred.

We both pulled hard. The bateau ran out past the island. Looking over our shoulders, we could see the high antlers and just a hand-breadth of his black nose going steadily off from the Point. Faint splashes came to our ears.

"Steady," said Fred. "He has a good mile to go to get to the other shore. We are all right for him."

But the great beast swam powerfully; and he kept bearing away to the southward. Probably he had sighted our boat. We drove the bateau along at a right jolly rate; but we did not gain much. The moose was a full hundred rods in advance of us. We found that we should have to put out our strength, and settled down to it for a regular heat. We were earning the game. For the first quarter of a mile we had not perceptibly gained a rod. Then we buckled down to it; and the next time Fred looked he said we were nearing him.

But we neared very slowly; and if the creature had not kept sheering off from us, thus giving himself farther to swim, the chances are that he would have got away. But he tired himself down at length, and after the first three fourths of a mile we began to close up with him. The hundred rods shrank to fifty, and this distance to twenty, while yet he was a quarter of a mile from the southeast shore.

"Keep at it," Fred exhorted me; for I was getting nearly as badly blown as the moose himself.

"His head keeps going under water," Fred said to me.

I expect this was from the great weight of his antlers.

Fred would not stop to fire till we were close up to the creature, lest we might miss and allow him to get the start. It was not till we were so near that I could distinctly hear the labored breath of the animal, that my comrade pulled in his oars and seized one of the muskets. I stopped rowing to see the shot. Fred aimed at the back of the moose's head. At the report he jumped in the water, with a loud grunt that threw the spray in two jets from out his nostrils. Then he sank partially, but rose and swam again. I caught up the oars. Fred took up the double-barrelled gun and shot it twice more. One of these bullets, as we afterward found, passed through his head completely.

We were now close upon him; but, not knowing whether he was dead or not, we did not dare to approach too near. He had ceased to swim, and, as we watched, sank down so far, that even his antlers went nearly out of sight.

"He's dead, I know," Fred said; "and if we don't take him, he will sink to the bottom, and we shall lose him."

With a couple of strokes, I sent the bateau close upon him; and Fred caught hold of the top prongs of the antlers.

He said that even then he could feel a thrill of his expiring life through them.

We drew the carcass up to the stern; and, getting a noose about the antlers with our tow-line, drew his head entirely above water, and made it fast to the ring.

We then took breath.

We had got our moose; but we had not got him home, by any manner of means, as we soon began to realize; for, on taking the oars for our return pull, we found that the carcass towed unconscionably hard. Fred declared that it was like towing a raft of logs. It seemed to me like a ship dragging her anchor. There was no help for it, either, unless we cut loose from him altogether, and that we did not want to do. At best, we could only move at a snail-pace; and the labor was so fatiguing, coming as it did on the end of our race down the lake, that we were obliged to rest at intervals of ten minutes.

Some idea of the task we had to tow the carcass up to camp will be obtained, when I state that we were from a few minutes after eleven till near four o'clock getting back with it. Even after entering the stream, the hoofs dragged on the bottom. It took in water, too, and was tremendously distended.

Farr had seen the chase from Indian Point: he had watched, and saw us kill the moose. Scott and he had long been expecting us. But when they came to help us pull him out of the water, they did not wonder at our slowness. All four of us had hard work to get the carcass out of the stream upon the bank.

The antlers of this moose were two feet and seven inches high as they grew out of the skull. There were two main branches, with eight minor branches, or prongs.

The entire length of his body was eight feet four inches; the height, to the tops of his withers, six feet five; the girth just back of his fore shoulders, six feet six inches (about).

His chest was exceedingly broad and heavy; his muffle very long and flexible.

It took but a slight knock of the axe to detach the antlers from the skull. It was getting toward the season of the year (December) when moose shed their antlers.

It is said that moose frequently knock off their antlers while running through the woods; and that, to cure the soreness of the exposed wound, they rub the firs to apply the balsam.

On one of the old axe-helves I found a two-foot measure laid off, with brass tack-nails driven into it. This I found useful in determining my measurements with the tow-line.

So exhausted had Fred and I become with our labor, hunting this moose, that we did nothing more for that day.

Farr and Scott skinned him, and afterward hung up the best parts of the meat inside our log-fort.

# CHAPTER XXV.

### THE OUTLAWS AGAIN.

THE snow melted somewhat during the afternoon; but as night came on, the wind grew very chilling and it began to freeze.

Farr and Scott moved the stove into the shed, cutting a hole through the roof for the rusty old funnel; and, in order to make our position as cosey as possible, they brought an immense mass of the long fan-like boughs, from the green tops of the spruces we had felled, and fairly overlaid our shed with it, shingling them on to the depth of several feet.

For supper, we had all we wanted of the moose sirloin, with roasted potatoes and Horsfords. The Cannucks had not used any of the bread preparation. Very likely they did not know what it was.

The morning following, Fred had the watch from half-past three till six; and at a few minutes before the time we generally got up he waked us, bidding us be quiet and come out without noise.

It was just beginning to get light a little. We crept out. Fred was on his knees, looking through a chink in the fence on the side next the river. I knew there was something in sight.

" What is it ? " Farr whispered.

" Cannucks," Fred whispered back.

That was a word that rendered us broad awake on the moment. We crept along and applied our eyes to the chink.

" Where ? " queried Scott.

" Look straight across the stream. About three rods from the bank. Right behind that big fir," Fred directed. " See him ? "

We looked attentively, anxiously; yet it was not at once, in the dim dawn, that I made out that there was a man standing behind the fir, with just a segment of his face visible, peeping from behind the trunk.   And it took Scott and Farr even longer to make him out.

"Only one?" I said.

"That's all the one I've seen yet," Fred said.   "The others may be back in the woods, waiting, while he reconnoitres."

"How long has he been standing there?" whispered Farr.

"About ten minutes," Fred said.

"I don't see how you came to see him at all," said Scott.

"In the first place I heard a stick snap off over there," Fred explained hurriedly.   "That set me to looking.   And a minute after I saw this chap steal along to this fir.   They are watching for a chance to pounce on us."

"Best to fire on him?" Farr questioned.

"I should not want to kill him," said Scott.

"No; we don't want their dirty blood on our hands," Fred said. "But it would be well to fire and scare him : let him know he cannot surprise us, and that we are up to all their tricks."

"The old double-barrel's loaded for partridges," whispered Farr. "The shot would not hurt anybody at that distance."

"Bring it on," said Fred, grinning.

Back crept Farr after the gun.

It was growing lighter.   We saw the concealed prowler turn and beckon with his hand, and immediately another figure came stealing cautiously forward from a tree a little farther off.   Then they both got on their hands and knees, and crept cautiously forward into a clump of alders not a rod from the river.   In the increasing light, I distinctly saw a silvery gleam from the nickel-plating on the skeleton stock of the little rifle.   Fred saw it, too, and nudged me.

"By Jove! I believe I could pick him from here with this musket," Fred whispered, "and stop that rifle from going away again!"

It was a temptation. The sight of our little " pet " in their hands made us feel revengeful.

" They would shoot us with it in a moment, if they could," Fred said.

Farr came back with his shot-gun.

" They 've got our little rifle there," Fred whispered.

" The thieves ! " muttered Farr, after an indignant look. " Let 's give them bullets ! "

But we could not bring ourselves to do that.

" No," Fred whispered. " We 'll shed no blood, unless we are obliged to do it in self-defence. That 's the best rule to go by. It would be a bad thing to have to think of afterward."

The two Cannucks were still crouching there in the alder clump. The distance was ten or twelve rods. We knew the bird-shot would not hurt them.

" Let it squirt at them," Fred whispered.

Farr cocked the barrels as easily as possible; then, just resting the muzzles in the chink, took aim, and discharged a barrel.

The flash and the sharp report broke the early morning quiet with startling suddenness. Instantly the two Cannucks jumped out of the alders and ran. We heard the oaths flying out of their mouths. Before they had got ten yards, Farr fired again; and Fred, pointing the old musket in the air, discharged that. We heard them heeling it off at a great pace through the brush.

It was vastly laughable. We lay there, and shook ourselves. We did not know whether they were really meditating an attack on our camp, or had merely come round to steal the bateau, which lay in the stream at the foot of the knoll. In either case, they got pretty thoroughly frightened.

" They won't be seen round here again to-day," said Fred. " It will take them about forty-eight hours, I reckon, to get their courage sworn up to the fighting-point again. They will have to swear over their whole vocabulary of profanity and obscenity, and add a few new oaths to it, before they will be in plight to come round again."

That day Fred and I went the round of the "saple" line and the traps down at the dam. They were badly filled with snow. We had a stint to clear them out and set them in order.

"Trapping is poor business after snow comes," Fred kept saying. "The sooner we give it up, and go to digging gum, the better."

There was one marten caught near the southwest corner of the lake; nothing in the mink traps at the dam or on the rapids below.

It was sunset before we had made the entire round, and got back to camp. The snow made the walking more than usually difficult.

Farr had been down to the musk-rat traps in the cove. There were four rats caught. Our profits that day were too meagre to be encouraging; but we had plenty of moose-meat.

That night there was another prowler about, of a different sort. It was getting dusk. Farr had taken the pail to get some water for tea. We brought our water from the stream at the foot of the knoll, where the bateau was moored. To avoid the more stagnant water near the bank, we used to step into the boat and dip it over the side. Farr was just about to step from the shore into the boat with the pail, when a snap of twigs caught his ear; twigs snapping were ominous sounds with us in those days. It seemed to come from the bank a little above and up the stream. He glanced quickly, hearing the brush crack, and saw through the bushes, indistinctly, a long black object stealing down toward him.

With a yell Farr dropped the pail, and came up the knoll "at three jumps," to use his own expression. The rest of us were in the camp, where we had already lighted the basin-lamp; but hearing the outcry, we seized our guns and sprang out, just in time to see Farr dive in at the "sheep-hole."

Thinking there was an enemy in close pursuit, Fred and I leaped

WITH A YELL FARR DROPPED THE PAIL.

to drop the door; while Scott jumped upon the log platform, gun in hand.

"What is it?" Fred cried out, cocking his gun, and glancing alarmedly around.

"I dunno!" was Farr's lucid explanation; then he got up on the log platform beside Scott, and peered excitedly over the fence.

This did not make the matter very plain to the rest of us.

Said Fred, "I should like to know what's up, anyway, Farr."

"Well, I guess you'd have thought something was up," said Farr. "Didn't you see him, Scott?"

"I thought I saw something," Scott admitted; "but it darted away like a shot."

"Well, it came like a shot, you'd better believe," said Farr. "The first I saw of it, it was crouching almost to the ground, and coming like a dart. I came up this hill at just three jumps, and the thing was at my heels when I came in the hole."

"But what did it look like?" asked Fred, getting on the log platform, and glancing sharply about the camp.

"Well, I don't know exactly. It was long, and it looked dark-colored; and it came after me like a streak o' goose grease. By gracious! another foot, and it would have caught me, sure's you live! I didn't hear its feet at all;" this was about all Farr could tell.

"What did _you_ think it looked like, Scott?" persisted Fred.

"Why, it is so dusk, I could not see very well," said Scott. "It went out of sight among the spruce-tops so quick, I only barely got one glimpse of it."

"That must have been a queer animal," Fred laughed.

"'T was a confounded catamount!" exclaimed Farr: "that's what it was."

"Might have been, possibly," Fred said rather incredulously. "Wish I could have seen it, though."

"Well, I wish you could!" cried Farr, who did not quite like the humorous view of the chase in which the rest of us were indulging. "I should have been very willing to swap places with you just at that time; and if you've a mind to, you may go and bring that pail of water."

"All right," said Fred, and went and brought it.

Farr would not say anything more about it, because we laughed. But there really was something that made a dive at him. What it was, it was hard telling. As Fred said, it might have been a panther possibly; or it may have been a large and ferocious lynx, such as are sometimes fallen in with in this section. After snow comes and the weather gets cold, all wild creatures are more dangerous. Ever after that we were more cautious about going out after nightfall; but Farr's "streak o' goose grease" was always a pretty good joke.

# CHAPTER XXVI.

### UP A TREE.

THUS far, like the four animals in the fable, we had lived in the greatest peace and harmony; but the morning after this adventure we had a regular muss in camp.

Farr was cutting wood and bringing it into the camp, and Scott was getting ready to make some tea. He had poured water into the tea-pot, and, after rinsing it about, stepped to the doorway to throw out the "grounds;" and he threw them, water and all, just as Farr was coming in. The whole mess splashed in his face and all over him. Farr thought he did it on purpose; he dropped the wood and went at Scott by guess, not even giving him time to explain.

They clinched, and flew round there at a great rate; they were not quite angry, but pretty near it. It took Fred and me both to pull them apart. Farr had got hold of a handful of the grounds, and wanted to scrub Scott's face with them. It was a cold morning, and they both felt a little fractious. The fun of the thing afterward was, that Scott could never make Farr believe that he did not throw those grounds on purpose.

That day, or else it was the day following, we took up all the musk-rat traps. For several nights we had caught no more than one or two. We let the mink traps remain, however, and determined to tend the "saple" line a week longer.

Our other traps we set over at the unknown pond we had found the night we found the lynx. These we visited every second day; and it was while returning from one of these rounds that Scott and I had a lively adventure with some lynxes.

We had been round the pond, and were coming down the north-east side of it, when we came quite suddenly upon three of these creatures gnawing the bones of some animal. It was among brush and old spruce-tops. We were within ten yards of them before we saw them. They leaped up spitting when they saw us; and one of them, a hideous-eyed old male, began to yawl and miawl and arch his furry back at us. They were mad at being disturbed while eating.

Scott had one of the muskets, and instantly cocked it.

" Now knock the eyes right out of the big one !" I said.

He fired. They all sang out loudly at the report; and then the first thing we saw was the old Tom coming straight for us, snarling and snubbling like a dog when just going to join battle with another. The musket bullet (as we found afterward) had torn one of his ears nearly off.

Scott gave a warning shout, and sprang aside amid the brush, and ran as fast as he could. For my own part, I dodged behind a great basswood standing there, and jumped to a small white maple about a rod off. The cat was making for me, with his back up and his neck beautifully curved under and on to one side! The idea of a hand-to-hand combat with all three of them was not pleasant. I dropped the axe I had in one hand, and shinned up the maple at my best rate of climbing! It was not a hard tree to climb. I readily gained the first limbs, and swung one leg over a large one, — not much too quick either. The old lynx, maddened by the pain of his lacerated ear, ran vengefully up after me, his great claws cutting audibly into the bark, and showing some ugly long feline teeth. No time for reflection! I drew up my legs as snugly as possible, and, when the beast got within reach, kicked down with emphasis. The heavy boot-heel, armed with iron " buttons," gave a hard poke full on the creature's head. It relaxed its hold a little, slipped back a few feet, and then went sliding

THEY CLINCHED, AND FLEW ROUND AT A GREAT RATE.

and growling, with its claws tearing through the bark, to the foot of the maple again.

I expected another onset next breath, and drew up my foot for another kick. But the old brute contented himself by sitting down, as did also the other two, and staring evilly up at me out of their great silvery eyes!

The thought of tumbling down among them was not a relishable one. I watched them a few moments, and then hallooed for Scott, who I thought ought by this time to be putting in an appearance with the gun.

"Here I am, — out here!" responded my comrade, at a distance. "Where are the varmints?"

"Under the tree here, all three of them, looking up at me. Why don't you come and shoot 'em? — you're a pretty fellow to shoot a lucivee!" I could n't help flinging out at him.

"Why don't I come and shoot 'em!" repeated Scott, derisively. "How can I come and shoot 'em when you 've got the bullets?"

Sure enough, the little leather pouch of bullets was in my pocket, instead of his!

An embarrassing pause succeeded this discovery.

"Well, what are you going to do?" said I, at length.

"I 'm sure, I don't know," answered Scott.

There was another pause.

"I 'll tell you, Scott!" said I, after some thought. "You begin and creep up still, through the brush; and I will throw the pouch out to you. I can throw it thirty or forty yards off over their heads. You will see and hear it when it falls; then you can creep up sly, and get it."

"Not if I know myself!" cried Scott, at once rejecting this proposal. "They 'll see me and take at me! Then *I* shall have to climb a tree."

"But you really ought to do something for a fellow," said I, rather injuredly.

" I know that," said Scott; "and the only thing to be done is to go back to camp and get some more balls or shot."

" Well, do go as quick as you can, and get Fred," I exhorted. " It's rather hard roosting up here."

He went away; and I settled myself as best I could among the limbs. But it *was* hard roosting: it was not a good tree to roost in. The branches left the main trunk at a very acute angle. It grew fearfully tiresome holding on up there. I hoped the cats would go away. If I kept quiet, I presumed they would go back to the carcass, where we had disturbed them; and one of them did go back. Presently I heard it gnawing the bones. But the other two kept under the tree, and stared steadily up at me. The old male that Scott had hit continued to flip his wounded ear, and grumble bitterly to himself. The pain was just enough to keep him angry.

It was getting dusk; Scott had been gone almost two hours; and I was nearly paralyzed in my cramped and tiresome perch, when I heard Fred call out cautiously, and at some distance.

I thankfully responded.

" I 'm coming," said he. " We 've got three guns loaded with buckshot. I 'll fix 'em now."

" Yes," said I, " pepper them good; but don't shoot into the tree."

Very cautiously he made his way from one tree-trunk to another, till he got up within sight and range of the lynxes; then, crouching behind a log, cocked one gun and laid it beside him ready, and taking careful aim with the other, fired both barrels at once. A squall from the lucivees followed the report. They leaped up, as the large shot cut through their hides. The next moment Scott fired at them, — a good shot. The old male dropped; the other was leaping about, miawling loudly. I began to slide down the tree ; and Fred, running up, knocked the wounded lynx on the head with the gun-stock. The other one had skulked off at the noise of the firing.

So rigid had my joints become from holding on so long, that I could scarcely step for some minutes.

We skinned the two lynxes. The carcass of the animal they had been eating when we came upon them seemed, from the black hair of the bits of skin that lay about with the bones, to have been that of a small bear. Whether it had died of itself, or the lynxes had killed it, we could not tell. We had never heard of these animals attacking a bear. Still, it is not impossible that they may have done so. The old male was very large and fierce.

His skin brought us seven dollars; that of the smaller one four dollars. We deemed that a pretty good day's work, on the whole.

# CHAPTER XXVII.

### FRED'S STRANGE ADVENTURE.

THERE came a number of warm and sunny days at this time. The snow nearly all went off.

We caught three more martens and two minks; and the fourth day after our adventure over at the pond Fred brought in an otter caught in one of the traps there.

Now, an otter had been one of our fairest dreams, and we felt a good deal elated. We expected from twelve to fifteen dollars for the skin, and, as a matter of fact, did get eleven dollars for it.

Fred came in, and threw it down without a word. Scott had never seen an otter. We made him believe it was a panther's kitten at first, till he got sight of its webbed toes.

The color of this otter seemed, at first sight, a deep wine-color; but on opening the long outer hairs, the fur was seen to be of a lighter tint.

Fred skinned and stretched it very carefully. Its black ears were very short, but broad; and its nose was very broad, or blunt. Its tail was long and very thick at the base, but tapered to a point. The fur of the tail, as also of the whole body, was very rich-tinted and glossy.

The entire weight of the animal may have been thirty pounds, — at a guess, not less than that. It was not, we thought, a very large individual.

Encouraged by this success, we carried over seven or eight more of the traps, and set them around the pond; and Farr and Fred set the large trap over in the "bear-path," where we had caught the lynx. Once the snow had come, we had noticed many tracks here; indeed, the forest was full of tracks. If one had judged from the tracks alone, he would have supposed that the woods were alive with ferocious beasts; for many of the tracks had a most formidable appearance. In running through snow, the lynx often takes eight and ten feet at a jump, and, striking all its feet together, makes the snow fly about smartly.

During this Indian summer weather we had begun to dig gum in good earnest. The woods on both sides of the lake offered plenty of gum for the digging. More than half of all the trees were spruces. It did not take long to hunt up one with gum on it.

Leaving a man to guard camp (we did not omit that duty), three of us would sally out with our guns, gumming-knives, hatchet, and the sacks we had contrived to put the gum in, and work steadily for five and six hours at a stretch. It is not so exciting a business as trapping; yet it is as pleasant, and, judging from our experience, far more profitable.

Spruce-gum, when of good quality, sells readily for a fair price in all our New-England cities. If a party of young fellows have only the grit to endure the hardship and rough life of the woods, they can do a very fair business at gumming round Parmachenee Lake. Of this fact I am confident. If they are diligent, they can safely expect to clear two dollars and a half per day. If we had gone into gumming in the first place, instead of trapping, we should have made double what we did. Gumming is a business you can safely count on from day to day. Trapping is just the reverse of this.

For a while we used to keep together as we gummed, and always laid our guns convenient. But as day after day went by without our seeing or hearing anything more of the Cannucks, we grew less cautious. We hoped and began to believe that they had left the vicinity, and that we should see nothing more of them. To carry a gun round with one constantly is a great task. At length we would take but one gun and the revolver, and take turns carrying the gun; and after a time we would get strayed apart. In such a business as digging gum it is very difficult for three to keep close together all the time. Often we would lose sight of one another altogether, and, after filling our sacks, return to camp alone and at different times in the afternoon.

We had been gumming in this way for a week or upwards, when an event happened that threw a sad gloom over us for many days, and showed us the necessity of constant care and precaution.

On the morning in question Farr had remained to guard the camp; and Fred, with Scott and myself, had gone over to the east side of the lake toward Moose Brook; and my own luck in finding good trees being unusually bad, I did not get back to camp till near dusk.

Scott had got in an hour and a half ahead of me. He and Farr had supper ready and were waiting, and had been looking for Fred and myself; they thought we might be together.

"Where's Fred?" was therefore the question with which they greeted me.

I had not seen him since a few minutes after starting out in the morning. No more had Scott, and Scott had carried the gun that day too; I had the pistol. Still, we supposed he would be in before long; and digging open the "bean-hole," pulled out the kettle of hot baked beans, and fell to work with prodigious appetites.

Meanwhile it was growing dark rapidly.. A chill, biting wind blew from the northeast; it was overcast and dreary.

Presently Scott started up, exclaiming, "Fellows, I'm worried about Fred! It's been in my head all day that something was going wrong with some of us. I don't see where he is all this time!"

We all felt pretty anxious. To be out after dark in the wilderness there was not safe.

"I guess we had better fire a gun," said Farr.

Our supply of ammunition was very scant. Scott drew the shot from one barrel of one of the shot-guns, and carefully put it back into the pouch; then, stepping out in front of the log shanty, he discharged it.

Farr and I listened intently. Save the quick, smothered echo, and the surge of the wind amid the tree-tops, there was no response. Then we hallooed repeatedly; then discharged the second barrel of the gun.

"He may have heard it," said Scott. "If he did, he will come in. We will wait awhile and see."

We waited ten or fifteen minutes; he did not come. We grew really alarmed.

"There's something wrong with him," said Scott. A chill fell upon us standing there.

"Fred isn't a fellow to stay off like this," Farr remarked. "He's either lost, or something's caught him."

We thought of the Cannucks.

"If he is lost, we must hunt him up if we can," said Scott, determinedly. "It's no more than he would do for any of us."

By this time it had grown dark, — the darkness of a cloudy night. Farr split up an armful of pitch-wood splints; Scott recharged the gun; I looked to the fire, and took one of the muskets. We then crossed the stream, and lighting two of the pitch-wood torches, entered the woods, taking the direction we had gone in the morning.

But it was blind work, picking our way among and over windfalls. Once I espied a marten staring at us from a mossy rock; but it vanished ere I could raise the gun.

A lynx saluted us with a long *yawl* at a little distance; but more dismal and annoying still were the *hoots* and *tu-whoos* of a couple of owls, that were attracted by our torch-light, and pursued us, circling and flapping among the fir-tops.

It began to spit snow, — snow and sleet commingled. We kept

on, however, for a mile or over, till we reached the height of land where the heavy spruce growth takes the place of the firs. Here we stopped and hallooed again and again; but the owls replied so provokingly that we could have heard nothing else. Scott fired at one of them, but missed it in the darkness. The sleet, too, made a dull, continuous rattling, as it fell through the branches.

It was of little use to search for him at that time of night. Our splints were already more than half burned. We went back; we were obliged to do it. The wind was cold, and the sleet pelted hard; it seemed as if winter was coming on.

I remember that we scarcely spoke. Our fears for Fred filled us with a strange gloom. We sat round the stove; not one of us closed his eyes that night.

As soon as it was light, we ate a few mouthfuls and set off. The whole forest looked snowy and odd in the gray light of that cloudy morning. There had fallen about an inch of snow and hail; it was slippery walking. We hurried forward, however, and went over the whole ground where we had gummed the previous day.

We had taken our guns, and did not get out of sight of one another; for the forest seemed fearfully wild and savage now that Fred had disappeared within it.

But we found nothing, and saw no trace or track of him; half hoping that he had come in, and that we should find him at the camp, we went back to it at noon.

He was not there.

In the afternoon we set off to make a wider circuit; and, almost running in our anxiety, we kept on for as much as seven miles to the southeast, and came round to the east and north, — in all, twenty miles without doubt.

We hallooed at intervals, and fired the gun several times, quite in vain. We did not find a trace of him.

" We shall never know what has become of him," said Scott.

The tears would come when we thought of that.

It was dusk before we got round to the camp; for we came near losing our way ourselves.

It was a sad thing to feel that we had done our best, and yet done nothing to bring him back.

Too sorrowful to eat much, we sat looking gloomily off into the darkening woods, when the cracking of the brush made us start. Through the fallen spruce-tops on the west side of the camp, something — a person — was coming at a headlong pace.

" It 's Fred — or his ghost ! " cried Scott.

We all ran out and called to him, as he rushed, or rather staggered, toward the camp. A sick thrill went through me as I looked at him. His clothes were torn. He looked wild and haggard. His eyes were blood-shot, and he cried out in a strange voice, " Fellows, *I 've been more than two hundred miles !* "

Then he threw himself flat on the ground, and sobbed and cried like a child. I took his hand, and put my finger on his pulse. It was fearfully quick. His flesh burned. He was on the verge of brain-fever.

We said not a word to him, but took him up and laid him in the bunk. Then Scott got lukewarm water, and we washed his feet, the bottoms of which were blistered and raw. After that we bathed his head in cold water, and washed his hands. He was utterly exhausted, and in about an hour dropped asleep, but kicked and muttered a good deal.

We watched him awhile, then fell asleep ourselves, for we were thoroughly fatigued.

Next morning Fred was calmer, but pitifully pale and hollow-eyed. We got him a warm breakfast of roast potatoes and toasted biscuit, and made him some tea. The food did him good; and he began to talk, though he could hardly speak of his hardships without shedding tears.

His account to us was like this : —

" I kept gumming, and going from tree to tree that morning, till I had dug my sackful, and thought, from my feelings, that it must be afternoon. It had come on cloudy. But I had not felt 'turned round,' nor anything of the sort, till I started to come back to camp. Then, all at once, it came upon me like a whirl, and for my life I could not tell which way to go ! It startled me a good deal ; but I kept cool. I laid down my gum-sack and hatchet, and climbed a yellow birch to the first limbs, about twenty-five feet, to take a look off. I was not fairly up above the spruce-tops ; but I saw a mountain, that I took for old Bose-buck, across the lake. So I broke a limb on the side next to it, and then slid down, took up my sack and hatchet, and set off in that direction. I was n't much uneasy ; I thought I was all right. I walked pretty fast, and after a while began to wonder why I did not come out at the shore of the lake. But I kept on for as much as fifteen minutes longer, with no signs of coming to the water.

" Then I knew that I must be going wrong ; the woods, too, looked different from that round the lake. I began to grow bewildered again, and climbed a white maple almost to the top. Not a sign could I see of a mountain anywhere, nor of the lake !

" The land rose in swells, covered with black spruce all about. I was down in a valley.

" You see, that was n't Bose-buck that I saw from the first tree. I was turned round then. Instead of Bose-buck, it was old Birch-board mountain, away up toward the Canada line.

" But I was n't certain of anything now. I got down out of the tree. My head began to whirl, and the strangest feelings came over me. There was a brook in the valley. I got down and drank from it, and bathed my forehead.

" That brook, I suppose, must have run out into the Magalloway. If I had had sense enough to follow the brook, I should have come out upon the river ; but I never thought of it, I was so confused.

THEN HE THREW HIMSELF ON THE GROUND, AND SOBBED LIKE A CHILD.

"I got up from the brook, and started the way it seemed to me the camp was, and ran just as fast as I could. I must have lost my gum-sack about that time; but I did n't know when I lost it. On I went; and the first thing I knew, I was whispering and jabbering to myself. My head began to ache as if it would split.

"All at once I came to a brook, took a drink, and stuck my head in the water; then jumped across, and ran on again as fast as I could; and in about fifteen minutes I came to another brook, just about as big as the other one, drank, and ran on again; and in a few minutes came to still another brook! And though I had drunk not ten minutes before, I was so parched with thirst that I flung myself down to drink again.

"As I was getting up, I saw a boot-track in the wet gravel and sand. I thought for a moment that I must be near where some of you were, or had passed. But, on looking again, I saw the mark of my iron button in the heel: it was *my own track!* *All those brooks* I had been coming to were the same. I had been running right round and round; and the last time I had come around to the same place exactly where I had jumped across the brook before.

"That thing scared me worse still. I was getting wild. I pulled my coat off and climbed another tree, — a large ash. But a mist had begun to fall; and it had grown so dusk that I could not see much. I got down, and started on, with my back to the brook; and every large tree I passed I gave it a 'spot' with the hatchet; and that, or something else, kept me from circling, for I did not come to the brook again.

"I think, perhaps, that I had gone three or four miles from this brook, when I heard a twig snap behind me. I looked round, and could just make out something in the dusk seven or eight rods away. I had raced about so much that some creature had got on my track. I was so desperate and wild that at first I did not care for it. But I kept looking back, and the more I thought of it the more alarmed I grew ; for I knew that after it got dark the beast might spring upon me, and that I ought to build a fire.

"I had matches in my pocket ; and the next pine stump I came to I split off a lot of shivers with my hatchet, and kindled a blaze.

"As soon as I got a light started I could not see about me as before ; but every few moments I could hear the snap of some dry branch, now on one side and then on the other. The animal was hanging about, — walking round the fire. That was not a very pleas-ant thing to know. I had no idea what it was. I sat down between the fire and the stump, and hewed off splinters to keep the blaze bright, and cut up a small sapling of white birch to make brands ; so that after that, whenever I heard the brute's step off in the brush, I would let a brand fly in that direction.

"Two or three times I heard it jump aside when the brands fell near it ; and once I thought that I heard it snarl.

"Two or three hours passed. Despite my fear of the prowling animal, I began to grow very drowsy from fatigue. I had several bushels of chips cut off ; and I now placed my back to the stump, and stretched my feet out to the fire. Every few minutes I would throw on a handful of the dry chips. I must have dropped asleep while sitting there, for suddenly I jumped to my feet. The fire was nearly gone out, and I had a glimpse of a wild, ferocious head, with gleaming eyes, scarcely a rod away, that drew back into the darkness as I stirred. The beast was stealing upon me.

"This startled me so much that I did not go to sleep again. It was cold, too. A good deal of hail and snow sifted down through the tops of the spruces. It rattled drearily among the branches, and fell into the blaze of my chip-fire with spiteful hisses.

"Once after this, when the fire had waned a little, I heard the animal not far off; but as I immediately threw on more chips, and thumped lustily on the stump with the hatchet, it did not approach nearer ; and during the latter part of the night it must have gone away, for I heard nothing more of it; and when, at length, day broke, it was nowhere in sight. There was, however, a beaten path of tracks in the snow and hail around the stump and fire, at a distance of about a hundred feet. Some of these were nearly as large as the print of my hand in the snow.

"As soon as it had got fairly light, I started forward again with my back to the lightened east, for I supposed that our camp must be to the west of where I then was.

"To appease my hunger I chewed a great quid of gum, which I dug from a spruce. But I felt very weak, and had to stop often and lean against a tree to rest myself.

"During the forenoon I crossed a large brook, by wading through it at a place where the bottom was sandy, and then continued on for an hour or two beyond it, when it occurred to me that this great brook might be the upper course of the Magalloway. The more I thought about it, the more certain I felt of it. So I tacked, and took a direction which I believed would bring me back to it at a point considerably below where I had crossed it. I did not come to it so soon as I had expected, however.

"The afternoon was passing. I grew bewildered again, and soon got as wild and feverish as I had felt the night before.

"In this way I wandered on for two hours or over; and it had begun to grow dark again, when I caught sight of your fire, and came out to the camp and the river."

Such was Fred's story of his " two-hundred-mile " tramp.

It was nearly a week before he was strong enough to go out with us into the woods again.

# CHAPTER XXVIII.

WE made a solemn promise then and there never to lose sight of one another again while off in the woods. And indeed there cannot be too much care used.

During this following week Farr and I gummed alone, Scott, by voluntary offer, remaining at camp with Fred.

Saturday we varied the programme by going down the lake into Bose-buck Cove with the bateau, and thence down to Sunday Pond to our old den at the lower, end of it, in order to get the gum and other property left there.

While we were down there we had dug what we estimated at twenty-three or four pounds, and for five days that week we brought in what we called six pounds apiece each day. That was our stint.

We dug nothing but good gum. In the evening we would scrape and clean it nicely, then put it up in packages or boxes made of birch-bark, strongly sewed together with small roots of spruce. These we found very tough, though pliant, and more useful for our purpose than the twigs of yellow birch, which are sometimes made use of.

These long, tough spruce-roots are what the Indians use for sewing their canoes and for winding the gunwales.

We used to go over occasionally to look to our traps at the pond we had discovered. But we did not succeed in entrapping another otter, though we caught one mink.

For more than a week, too, nothing disturbed the large trap in the bear-path. Farr and I had got sick of going over to it for nothing, and set off determined to take it up and have done with the bother of it, when, considerably to our surprise, we found it gone, and the bait we had lavished about it all eaten up.

As before, we had attached two clogs to the traps. These made a very distinct trail, which we followed for a mile or more, to the foot of a steep ridgeside to the northward. Here a large spruce had blown partially over, raising a great mass of earth, scurf, and brush with the roots, and leaving a dark hole underneath them. The creature with the trap and clogs had taken refuge here. Indeed, the cavity was large enough to "drive in a flock of sheep," as Farr described it. It was a dark hole, too. We could not see much inside it. All was quiet about it, yet we did not care to get too near. Whether the creature was a lynx, a bear, or a panther was not certain, though we presumed that it was a lynx.

We had the hatchet with us; and with this Farr cut a long pole,— twenty feet at least,— and began to prod inside, to stir up the game. To the first three or four punches there was no response; but on trying the other corner of the den, there came a snarl so loud and vicious that Farr dropped the pole, and we both retreated to a safe distance. The trap-chain rattled. Evidently the game was alive and kicking.

"I don't see how we're going to get him out," Farr said, after we had considered the situation.

At length we concluded to fire under the root at a venture. Taking aim at what seemed to me the probable nook in which the beast was lurking, I fired first one barrel, then the second.

The only effect of this was to make the besieged brute growl ferociously.

We went around the root, and beat on it with the pole; but the creature would not run out.

We discovered, however, that the mass of dirt and dried leaves on the root was not very thick, and set to work to dig a hole through it on the back side. Cutting some short stakes, which Farr sharpened at one end, we fell to tearing away the earth, and at length got a small hole through into the cavity beneath. But no sooner had our stakes broken through, than, with a clank and rattle, the animal bounded out on the other side and went off on a leap, jerking the trap and clogs after it. It was as black as a crow.

"A bear!" I exclaimed, catching up the gun.

"Too small for a bear," Farr said.

We ran on after it. But, even encumbered as it was, it went off at a round rate; and we should have had a chase to come up with it, had not one of the clogs caught under a beech-root, bringing the creature up short. There it hung, springing and jerking, till, hearing us coming up behind, it suddenly turned, facing us with a harsh growl of defiance.

There it stood at bay, its eyes flashing, its body crouched close to the ground, its short ears cocked, and the long black hair along its back standing up like bristles. It was as large as a lynx, but had short legs.

Farr fired at it with a heavy load of buckshot. It went heels over head, but immediately got on its feet again, wheezing and growling, — a bloody and piteous spectacle.

Farr then stepped up, and fired the second barrel full at its head. It fell, but kicked a long while, dying very hard.

It was about the same weight of the lynx.

Farr carried the carcass, and I carried the trap.

On arriving at camp, Fred at once pronounced it to be a *fisher*, or fisher-cat, as some hunters call them, — an animal of the weasel family (*Mustela Canadensis*).

The creature is sometimes spoken of by naturalists as "Pennant's marten." Its color was black all over its body, save a few white hairs on its belly; its tail was rather long and shaggy; its legs were remarkably short, but stout; it had broad feet, and sharp black claws. Its teeth were as long and sharp as those of the lynx.

For its skin we received six dollars and fifty cents at our general sale.

It came on very cold that night. The stream froze, but there was too much wind to permit of the lake freezing. The next day, too, was cold and chilling. We shivered as we gummed. That following night it came on colder still. Shortly after midnight the wind lulled. I had the watch from half-past three till six in the morning. It was stinging cold. We were not surprised, as day broke, to see that the lake had skimmed over.

" How are we ever going to get out if the lake freezes up ? " Scott queried.

" Oh ! go down on the ice," Fred said.

" But how about our boat ? " I said.

" We 'll put it on runners," Fred laughed.

We were glad to hear him laugh again ; for he had had a sober time of it.

The next day he went out gumming with us for the first time since his misadventure. And I think it was that same day that we found a mink in one of our traps up at Little Boy's Falls.

The weather continuing very cold, the lake froze still harder, till it was like a huge mirror of plate-glass set in its black shores.

It was a grand chance for skating, — if we had had skates and the time for it. As it was, we gummed on steadily.

Our food was three quarters moose-meat.

Friday night of that same week, — about the 24th of November this was, — Farr called me up a few minutes after eleven o'clock, and waked Fred at the same time.

" There 's a Cannuck down at the ox-camp," he whispered to us. We did not wake Scott, but taking our guns, went out with Farr.

There was a moon again now on its second quarterage. It was just setting off over the spruces, but threw a bright light down into the opening below us. The ox-camp was plainly visible, so also the space about it, the frozen stream, and the blackened ruins of the burned camp.

We looked, but saw nothing.

"He's gone into the camp," Farr said, "or into the grain-shed. Hark!"

We distinctly heard a noise, a rattling of boards, and a sound as of pounding with a stone or a hammer.

"He's in there after our fur," I suggested. "Thinks, perhaps, we may have left those musk-rat skins or that lucivee's hide down there."

The noise continued louder than ever.

"He must be a fool," Fred said, "or else he does n't know we are up here. He must know that such a racket as that would wake us up."

Bump-bump! pound-pound! we could hear him knocking at something or other.

"Well, now, he is n't a bit afraid of making a noise, is he?" exclaimed Fred, wonderingly. "Just as lief we would know he is breaking in there as not!"

It struck me as a very strange performance. We could not imagine what sort of job he was at.

"You don't suppose it's a trick," Fred queried, "to get us out after him, and have his friends rush in and take our camp?"

"Like as not," Farr said.

We went round the camp inside our fence, and looked sharply off on all sides, but saw nothing of any lurking party. Still, they might be hidden among the brush in the shadow.

"Let him pound," said Fred; "we will stay where we are."

On a sudden the man came out of the grain-shed. We watched him attentively. He came along to where there was a stump, about a dozen yards from the shed-door. He had something in his hands, and set himself down on the stump.

"MUST BE HUNGRY," SAID FARR.

Pretty quick — so still was the air — we heard a sound of smacking.

"He's eating something," Fred said.

He was certainly eating. We could now see him raise a considerable piece of something or other, and tear off mouthfuls from it.

"Did we leave anything fit to eat down there?" I said.

"Nothing there but that barrel of sprung pork," Fred replied. "And I believe, upon my soul, he has broken in the head of that, and got out a chunk of it. That's the noise of pounding we heard."

"Must be hungry," said Farr.

"*Hungry!* I should think so," said Fred. "Why, I would as soon eat carrion as to eat that stinking stuff raw!"

"Well, that's what he's up to, sure as you're born!" exclaimed Farr. "Best to let a charge of shot fly at him?"

"No," said Fred. "Oh, no! he is welcome to that sprung pork, for all of me."

A minute later the moon went out of sight altogether, behind the thick green tops; and it grew too dusk even to see the outline of a man so far (fifteen or twenty rods). But we could hear smacking going on for fully twenty minutes longer. The fellow, whoever he was, was clearly making a square meal.

Once, some ten or fifteen minutes subsequently, we heard the crack of brush on the farther side of the stream to the east of our camp.

"He's going off, I guess," Farr conjectured.

We sat up with Farr an hour longer, I think; then, hearing nothing more of the mysterious pork-eater, we turned in again.

The next morning this midnight raw-pork eater was the subject of conversation. It puzzled us completely. We did not know what to think, — unless some of the Cannucks had in reality got starved out.

We went down to the ox-camp, and found, as we had suspected, the head of the barrel broken in with one of the old axes lying there. Otherwise the hungry man had left no trace.

Fred was on guard-duty that day.   Farr, Scott, and I gummed on the hills to the northwest of the lake.

There was a snow-squall near sunset; but the evening cleared up pleasant, with a broader and larger moon.   I had the first watch; and at about ten o'clock I heard something moving through the bushes and brush on the east side of the river.   It was going down the east bank.   I watched sharply, and a few moments after saw a man come out on the ice, and cross the stream at a point directly opposite the ox-camp.   He went straight to the grain-shed.   We had fastened the door with a nail; but the man broke it open readily and went inside.

Fred and Scott had not yet gone to sleep.   I stepped into our camp and spoke to them.

"It's the same one, no doubt," Fred said, "come back after another pork supper."

This time the "hungry man" was not long getting what he wanted. Immediately he reappeared with what we took to be a piece of pork, and going to his old perch on the stump, began to eat it.

"Well, does n't that beat the Dutch?" Fred exclaimed.

"We've got him for a regular boarder, or rather, Brown has," Scott said.

There was something so strange about this unknown person and his habits, that we felt queer as we watched him.

"He has no gun with him, no weapon of any kind," Fred remarked.

"But he may have a pistol," Scott suggested.

Yes, he might have a pistol.   We could not see him plainly; though the light was brighter than on the previous evening, we could yet do little but make out the form and figure of an ordinary-sized man.

After eating his pork he sat still awhile, then got up, stared around for a minute, and then stretched himself, or at least seemed to do so; for he raised his arms over his head in a slow and peculiar manner.

Pretty quickly he turned, and going down to the river, crossed on the ice, and entered the bushes on the farther bank. We heard him going off through the woods.

We watched awhile. Then Fred took my place, for it was his turn; Scott and I went to bed.

We were so completely mystified as to this strange person and his movements, that we did not now like to talk of him. The weird singularity of his comings and goings tormented us with a thousand fancies.

The next night he came a little after eleven, so Farr reported next morning; he had not thought it worth while to wake the rest of us.

We were beginning to get prodigiously curious to know something about him.

Said Fred at breakfast that morning, "I'm bound to find out who and what he is."

"If we should go down there when he is there, he might fire at us with his pistol, or draw a knife on us," Scott observed. "And if he is really so hungry as to come every night after that raw pork, why, I for one do not grudge it to him, though perhaps Brown might," he added, with a laugh.

"Tell you what we might do, fellows," Farr said. "We might hide there in the old ox-camp. Then we could take a square look at him, if he comes again. He doesn't go into the ox-camp at all: he makes straight for the pork-barrel in the grain-shed."

We determined to do it.

That day I recollect we got a marten, and found a musk-rat in one of our traps down at the dam.

Farr, Scott, and Fred made the round of the "saple" line, and gummed on the west side of the lake. I was on guard-duty. It was a quiet day. My comrades did not get in till dusk; and it was after eight before we finished supper and had skinned our fur. Immediately this was done, however, we loaded the guns afresh; and then Fred and Farr and I went down to the ox-camp, to lie in wait for our nocturnal visitor.

Inside the old camp it was dark as pitch. The moon was just coming up over the tree-tops as we went down. Soon the little clearing was all aglow with the silvery radiance.

We set an old grain-box six or seven feet within the door, in such a manner that one sitting on it could see out readily, while the darkness inside the closed camp would prevent his being discovered from without. On this long box we seated ourselves with our feet hanging off it, and began our vigils, or rather I should say that Farr and I sat on the box; for Fred stood in the door-way the most of the time on the lookout.

An hour or two passed. It was rather chilly, moping there. But our curiosity to solve the mystery kept us up to the mark of watching, though fully another hour passed before Fred at length exclaimed, "He's coming, I believe! I can hear the brush crack!"

Then we listened intently. Something was coming down the farther bank of the stream. A moment after, we saw him come out on the ice, and retreated back into the darkness, so that he might not discover us. We expected to hear his steps on the chips before the camp, but we heard not a sound of them; and the form of the man passed suddenly — before we were looking for it — into the grain-shed, without our getting more than a glimpse. So we drew forward as near the door as we dared, and looked for him to come out.

We could hear him pulling over the sprung pork; and anon he emerged and went directly to the stump, as before. Instantly I was startled by his odd looks.

"Good heavens!" Fred whispered. "*That's the Devil himself!*"

His hair, as we could now distinguish, was long, very long, and straggled in a tangled mane all over his face and shoulders. He had no hat. His arms were bare as high as his elbows, where began the tattered sleeves of his coat. His feet and legs were bare, too, up higher than his knees, to where the ragged skirts of his old coat covered them. Indeed, the only garment he seemed to have on was that tattered coat, — apparently an overcoat in its day, but now hanging in rags about him.

His arms, in the moonlight, looked brown and roughened. He held the great chunk of white pork in his black hands, and tore at it, animal-like, with his teeth; and, as he ate, he champed like a hog!

A strange feeling came over me as I looked at him: I felt sick at heart. It was a spectacle to disgust the intellect!

As he chewed and tore at the meat, his long, stringy hair flew about his face; and it was this hair that added so much to the strangeness of his mien.

"I do believe it's a woman!" Farr whispered.

"If it isn't Old Nick himself, I shall be thankful," said Fred.

"You don't suppose it is a wild man?" I whispered to Farr.

Farr said that he looked wild enough for that or anything else.

He sat with his back partially to us, so that we could not get a good view of his face.

After he had devoured the pork, he went off as he had come.

We went back up to camp to tell Scott.

"I've heard stories of a sort of woods-devil, like what we've just seen," Fred said. "The lumbermen and 'drivers' are always telling of such things. I supposed they were lying; but I begin to believe them."

"Nonsense!" said Scott. "I don't."

But we none of us knew what to think of it. Strangely superstitious feelings crept over us; the more we thought of it, the more unsettled we felt: it was like a nightmare.

# CHAPTER XXIX.

## "WE OUGHT TO KILL HIM!"

THE next night the "hungry man" came at a little past twelve. Fred had the watch. He waked Farr. They told us next morning that they had set out to fire at him, and either kill him or scare him off.

"If it's the Devil, *we ought to kill him!*" Fred said; and this shows what a bad hold the thing had taken on our minds.

Scott was more sensible.

"That's a human being," said he, "as much as we are. To shoot him would be murder."

Farr said that if it was a human being, it was the queerest specimen that ever he saw; for his part, he believed it to be a woods-witch, and if we did not look out it would bewitch us.

Scott ridiculed this talk.

"I'll be one of three to go down there and catch him," said he. "It's some poor woodsman who has got lost, and perhaps turned light-headed."

Fred admitted that he had heard of these cases, where men had got lost in these forests, and become crazy from wandering about. But he declared that he did not care to be one of the three to catch him. He should be very loath to lay hands on that creature, he said; should be afraid he might vanish, leaving a smell of brimstone behind him.

"Oh, what stuff that is!" Scott exclaimed in derision.

Thus we talked of it.

Of one thing we were pretty confident, — namely, that he had no weapons.

The next night Scott tried to induce us to go and help catch the man.

" If he 's crazy, wandering about here, we ought to do something about it," he argued. " By and by he will freeze to death, as the weather gets colder."

But he could not bring Fred or Farr to see it in that light at all.

" I guess he will manage to keep warm," Fred would say. " Looks to me like a chap that would not have any difficulty in finding a hot brick 'most any time."

" Humph !" Scott would exclaim. " What 's the use to be a fool, Fred ? "

Evidently the many stories that Fred had heard from the lumber-men had not been without some effect on his mind. He declared that he was not afraid of the man, but he did not mean to interfere with him.

Scott, on the other hand, argued that it was our duty to find out what ailed this person, and assist him. That very evening he roasted a piece of moose-meat in the oven, and taking it down to the grain-shed, hung it up, by a bit of rope, directly in the door-way. It was his watch (the first watch) that evening, and he watched till one o'clock (two watches) to see what came of it.

Next morning he told us that at a little before twelve the man had come ; and that on espying the roast meat hanging there, he had seized upon it with strange, wild exclamations of what Scott took for delight.

Fred told him that he had better not go to holding communications with the Devil.

But Scott now gave us no peace ; and during the next two days, first I, and then Farr, agreed to help him catch the unknown ; and at length Fred consented to help.

For my own part, I had by this time very little fear that it was a supernatural being; but I did dread to touch the poor filthy creature.

Accordingly, that night at ten o'clock we all four went down to the ox-camp, and hid ourselves there in ambush, as before. And this time we did not have long to wait. We had not been there more than fifteen or twenty minutes before we heard him coming through the brush on the other side of the stream.

" He 's more prompt since he has got a taste of your moose-meat, Scott," Farr said.

The strange being came up to the door of the grain-shed, looked about it awhile, then went inside. We held ourselves in readiness.

" Disappointed that he did n't find one of your moose-steaks waiting for him there," Farr whispered.

Presently the wretched creature came out with a piece of pork, and sat down on the stump.

Said Fred, " I had rather tackle a catamount than go near him."

" What foolishness ! " Scott whispered back. " The bare fact of his eating that pork shows that he is human fast enough."

" Don't know about that," retorted Fred. " Perhaps he needs it to grease down his brimstone with ! "

" Well, come on," Farr whispered. " If we must, we must. Now for him ! "

We had laid down our guns, and at the word made a rush at the unconscious pork-eater. But I must needs confess that we did it with no great alacrity. I think that each one of us was very willing that some of the rest should be the first to lay hold of him. We had but a few yards to go, and were upon him before he had even time to turn. Had we seized him pluckily on the instant, we should have held him beyond doubt; but we all held back a little.

Up leaped the unknown.

" Whooh ! " he snorted. " Moon-tykes !  Moon-tykes ! "

WE GAVE CHASE HARD AFTER HIM.

Scott seized hold of him; so did I, and so did Farr. But the man whirled, kicked, and struck with such effect that he threw us off and ran.

But now that our blood was up and we were fairly into it, we gave chase hard after him, — Fred ahead. Down the bank, on to the ice, and across the stream went the "hungry man," screaming " Moon-tykes! Moon-tykes!" at every leap. Half-a-dozen times going across the river we had our hands on him — almost. The opposite bank was three or four feet high, and set thick with alders. Among these the man leaped; but before he could force his way through them Fred grabbed him, and threw him back upon the ice. We all lay hold of him, by guess, but it was slippery as glass there. Round and about we went, and all came down together — wallop! I, for one, had both hands fastened into that old coat, and held on. But the coat did not hold the wearer! It gave way like brown paper. The pork-eater jumped out of it, and regained his legs. Fred seized one ankle; and the wretch ran, dragging Fred, stomach down, on the ice. His bare feet stuck, while our boots slipped. Fred said that the man kicked him in the head, and for that reason he let go his ankle. At any rate he got away, and ran off up the stream for twenty rods or more, and thence into the woods — *naked as when he was born!*

"I guess he will freeze to death now!" said Fred, as we listened to his departing footsteps.

Scott was disposed to blame the rest of us for not holding him.

"We had better have let him alone than used him in this bungling way," he said.

Farr laughed as if it were a good joke.

We hung his coat up on the alders, so that if he ventured back after it he might take it.

But next morning there hung the coat! I went down to take a look at it by daylight.

Of all the coats I ever set eyes on, that was the *shockingest* one!

It was a mere bunch of rags, filthy and malodorous to the last degree. I thought that it might originally have been of black tricot; but indeed it was hard telling what it was originally. The pockets had been torn out, or worn out, long previously. There was n't a single button on it. In front it looked as if it had been tied together with strings.

We watched the following night from ten till after one. The " hungry man " did not come; and next morning there hung his coat still. We never saw so much as a hair of him afterward.

Farr said that as he had nothing to wear, he was probably too modest to pay us another visit.

Scott regretted the way the affair had turned; he talked of little else for several days.

Three nights after, the old coat either blew away, or else the owner did actually come after it. And the man may even have come back to the grain-shed after more pork, for the moon did not now rise till toward morning, and cloudy weather had set in. As to who or what he really was, we never knew further than I have related.

At present writing, I am inclined to believe that it was a person more or less light-headed, — very possibly one of the Cannuck gang we had known of, whom the others had unfeelingly turned adrift to shirk for himself. The existence of several of these roving gangs is a well-ascertained fact. Sometimes they have plundered the fields, and stolen horses from the pioneer towns and plantations. The Moose-river settlement were seriously troubled by a party of nine of these woods-thieves only recently. Six or seven horses were taken, and the gang was dispersed and driven off only after a sharp and bloody fight with the citizens.

# CHAPTER XXX.

## SPECKLED BEAUTIES.

A FEW days later there came a snow-storm, heavy for that season. As many as seven or eight inches fell in one night. Our boots had worn almost entirely out. Scott had rubber boots, but the rest of us went with wet feet for three days in succession. We took cold by it, and felt miserable enough.

At length we determined to sacrifice one of our moose-hides and make it into moccasins. This we did, though they were not of any particular pattern, being mere oblong pieces of the hide folded over our old boots, hair side out, then bound tightly around our ankles.

Meantime we gummed on perseveringly; and another week passed.

Quite unexpectedly we now struck a new branch of business. I think it was Monday night of that week that Fred proposed to try the lake for trout, through holes in the ice. There were trout in the stream, and he did not see why there might not be trout in the lake.

We all hailed this project with delight. To tell the truth, we had become a little tired of gumming so steadily and so long. A change of business, even for a single day, was pleasing.

The next morning we were early astir. Farr lamented that fate gave him the duty of guarding camp that day; the rest rejoiced, I fear.

Directly after breakfast we got out our stock of fish-hooks and lines (including several stout hooks we had taken from the Cannucks).

" What shall we have for bait? " Scott questioned.

" Pork," said Fred.

"Not that sprung pork?"

"Yes; they will not mind it."

Farr suggested moose-meat.

We decided to take both, and wrapped up a generous chunk of each in one of the Cannuck waistcoats. Then, providing ourselves with a couple of the axes to cut holes in the ice with, we set off.

"Aren't you going to take something to bring your fish home in?" Farr called after us. "Better take the pail and the big pot!"

"You just attend to your duty," Fred retorted; "we'll attend to the fish. We don't mean to tempt Fortune to disappoint us by carrying a large dish."

"You're a superstitious fellow, Fred," laughed Scott.

We followed down the stream on the ice, and went out on the lake to a point directly between the first and second islands, this being the channel of the river in its course through the lakes.

"Guess we'll try 'em here," Fred said. "They will be more likely to be passing back and forth here than in dead water."

There was about six inches of snow on the ice. This we scraped aside; then Fred began to hack through the ice. It was no great job at this season. The ice was not over four inches thick; later in the winter — February, say — the ice would be found nearly a yard in depth. To cut a fishing-hole would then be a task, — half an hour of steady chopping.

Fred cut a small hole, eight inches in diameter.

"It isn't best to cut a too big one," he said. "We don't want one large enough to let ourselves through; else, if we should hook a big laker, he might do the catching part himself. That, you see, would not be pleasant."

"No," said Scott, "I should think not. They would soon pick a fellow's bones clean, those big trout, if he should tumble through here."

We agreed that it was not best to give the fish the advantage of a too big hole.

Meantime I had cut some stout alder sticks, about two feet in length, to the middle of which we made fast the ends of the lines, so that if dropped or twitched out of our hands, they might not be los through the hole into the lake. This done, Fred cut off a shred of the lean moose-meat, carefully baited his hook, and dropped it in at the hole.

Down it went, five, ten, a dozen feet; then he began to play it up and down after the manner of anglers generally.

Scott and I looked on expectantly. A minute passed, and no bite.

"Are n't hungry, I guess," Scott said.

"Loss of appetite," I hazarded.

"Froze up," Fred suggested.

"Gone a-visiting," Scott added.

"Moose-meat's too dark-colored," Fred observed. "Guess I will try the pork. That's whiter. See it better. Dark down there, perhaps."

He was drawing up the hook when there came a smart and most unexpected jerk. Fred jerked, too, and then held on.

"Got him?" we cried.

"Guess so," said Fred, carefully drawing in the line; "but he comes easy!"

All at once he did not come so easy; for the moment Fred brought the fish to the surface it made a sudden bolt off under the ice, pulling the line sharply through Fred's hands, and running out fully fifteen feet of it. Then began a sharp fight. To and fro went the strong fish, right and left, down and up, making the water fairly boil in the hole.

"Hold him, Fred!" we exhorted.

Fred held him easily enough; but a second later the fish drew the line against the sharp edges of the ice on the sides of the hole so forcibly that it frayed and snapped.

"Gone!" Scott cried out in a tone of anguish.

" Lost ! " I vociferated, fairly beside myself with grief for the moment.

"Gone, sure, hook and all," Fred said, examining his hands where the line had sawed into them.

" And now he will go and tell all the others," groaned Scott.

Fred took the axe and carefully smoothed the sharp edges of the ice around the hole.

"Ought to have done this in the first place," he said.

Then he prepared another line and hook, baiting it as before with moose-meat.

It had not gone down six feet before it was taken with a smart pull. This time Fred was on the lookout, and drawing the line quickly up, pulled out a fine large speckled trout, without giving it time to lunge and jerk. It came out quivering and struggling, the light flashing from its bright red spots.

Swinging it off from the hole, we let it flop a few moments, then unhooked it, and left it to die in the snow. It was a fine trout, and would have weighed two pounds and a half, we thought.

" Not so heavy as that first one," Fred said.

The fishes that we lose are the heaviest and finest, always.

Hardly had the hook been re-baited and dropped in again ere a third took it.

" If he told them, they don't heed it," Fred exclaimed.

" That 's the fate of good advice usually," Scott remarked.

This third fish was landed as quickly as the second. It was not quite so large.

" Going to have a streak of luck," Fred prophesied.

" Well, Frank," said Scott, " let us have a dab at it ! What 's the use to let Fred have all the fun ? "

" No use, clearly."

We seized the axes, and going off a little way, began to prepare each a hole for himself, into which we soon dropped our own hooks.

FRED PULLED OUT A FINE LARGE TROUT.

In a very few moments I had the fun, the rare sport, of pulling out a three-pounder, — the biggest one caught thus far!

I recollect the next two hours with delight, even now. It *is* fun to fish, when they bite well, and the mosquitoes do not bite too well. And we found Parmachenee Lake a rare good fishing-ground. We twitched out a lot of them that forenoon, and a very pretty lot too. All, save three or four chivin and one sucker, were speckled trout, weighing from a pound up to three pounds and a half. One we thought would have weighed four pounds. We soon had the snow about the holes lively with their frantic leapings.

Fred caught during that forenoon thirty-one, Scott got nineteen, and I got twenty-three: altogether, seventy-three. We thought that they would weigh near a hundred and fifty pounds. At any rate, there were about as many as we could in any way carry, all three of us. We strung them on large alder stringers, and went toiling back to camp under the weight of them.

Farr was astonished.

"How I wish I could have been there!" he bewailed.

We fried four for dinner, rolling them in meal to give them a good brown crust. They were delicious.

"What fools we were not to have fished there before?" Scott kept reminding us as we ate.

Toward four o'clock we went down again, and caught eleven more.

"I'm going to feed these holes," Fred said, "so as to draw a whole school of fish about them."

It seemed a good plan. We brought down a great quantity of the refuse moose-meat and unpicked bones, and dropped them into the holes, — to draw the fish.

"But what shall we do with all these trout?" Scott asked that evening.

"They're worth ten, twenty, and sometimes even fifty cents a pound in the cities, — these speckled trout," Fred said. "If the weather holds cold, I don't see why we cannot take these out with us and get something handsome for them."

Of course we all liked that idea.

Forthwith we got up one of the big grain-boxes from the grain-shed, and began to pack them down in clean snow.

The next morning we fished again at the holes. Farr tried his hand. Fred was on guard-duty. We caught twenty-four, and five more about sunset.

The next day we went down to the foot of the lake, — Fred and Farr and I, — and cut holes near where the outlet leaves the lake. Here we caught twenty-two, or about fifty pounds, as we reckoned it.

The day following, the other three boys fished both at the foot and the head of the lake: they caught seventeen.

That day the weather began to moderate. Toward night it came on cloudy. It looked like rain. We were anxious about our fish, lest they should spoil. We brought snow, and buried the box in it to the depth of two feet or over.

The next morning it was misty and wet. During the night there had been a most ominous groaning and roaring of the air beneath the ice on the lake, — a sure sign of a thaw, Fred assured us. All that day it held wet and warm. The snow melted considerably. But we kept a heap of it on the fish-box.

# CHAPTER XXXI.

## HOMEWARD BOUND.

THE next day was sloppier still. We used all the snow around to keep our box buried, and even cut slabs of ice out of the river. That night, however, about one o'clock, Fred reported a change. The clouds and fog broke up; the wind began to blow from the northwest. The next morning it was blowing smartly, and the damp snow and slosh on the ice was beginning to freeze.

"There's sure to be a hard crust," Fred said. "By to-morrow it will be gay running."

"And that means *Home!*" exclaimed Farr.

'T was a unanimous sentiment.

"Our fish won't stand another thaw, anyway," Fred said. "Let's be off."

We did not care to stay longer, and run the risk of being blocked in by a three-feet snow-storm. Evidently now was our time.

We fell to work to get ready. First, the bateau was cut out of the ice.

"Now, how can this be best turned into a sledge?" was Scott's question; and it was something of a question with the whole of us.

Fred went out and cut a stick of green white ash, twenty feet long. This, with the axes and with wooden wedges, he split in halves, for the runners. Then we knocked to pieces one of the old grain-boxes, to get nails. Along the flat bottom of the bateau we next nailed strips of hewn plank from the ox-camp, in two rows, lengthwise, and upon these we nailed the ashen runners, turning them up at the nose of the boat. The bottom of the bateau was then raised about four inches. At best it was a rather rough contrivance, but we could not then do better. This took till afternoon.

After dinner we loaded in the great fish-box, then the gum, next the fur, and afterward such of our remaining provisions as we might need, — a few frozen potatoes, a little meal, some of the moose-meat, and a few of the trout which we had saved out of the box.

That night we kept a vigilant watch, lest the Cannucks should come and steal our exposed treasures.

At six that next morning we ate our last breakfast at the fortified camp on the knoll. We had tea, trout, moose, corn-cake, and a batch of Horsfords. As soon as it was light we set off.

It was not without regrets that we bade adieu to our strong camp, where we had done sentinel duty for so many nights. One comes to love a place which he has to fight to hold.

Long before sunrise we had started down the stream. A faint wreath of smoke was rising from out the funnel of the stove, inside the fence, as we moved off. Farr even proposed to burn up the camp, that it might not fall into the hands of the Cannucks.

The tow-line was attached double to the nose of the bateau. Fred and I pulled, while Scott and Farr pushed. Altogether, it must have weighed near half a ton. But when once we had got it started on the ice, it ran almost of itself.

Instead of going down to the outlet, we went directly to the foot of Bose-buck Cove. Here we arrived a few minutes before nine. From this point we had determined to cut a road through to Sunday Pond, and thence out to the Little Magalloway. We had our own axe, and had also taken one of those at the ox-camp, for this purpose.

From the bottom of the cove to Sunday Pond it is about two miles. By carefully choosing our path where the woods were not very thick, we avoided cutting few trees larger than bushes. But it

was laborious work to drag the bateau through. It took all our strength. If there had been soft snow, we should never have got through. We were all the rest of that day getting down to the pond.

That night we camped at our old "den" at the foot of Sunday Pond. Tired enough we were too. We had only our tent, and such boughs as we could cut, for a shelter. We lay rather cold.

It took us all the next forenoon to get down to the Little Magalloway, — about a mile. Here we built a fire, and fried moose-meat and potatoes.

Once on the river, we found good sledding. The slosh on the ice had frozen hard as the ice itself. We had no trouble now in going on as fast as we could comfortably walk. A little later we came to the junction with the Magalloway proper, and during the afternoon went down through "the meadows."

Here it was that we again saw the robins eating round-wood berries.

In quite a number of places there was open water; but by keeping near the shore, on one side or the other, we got past with no great difficulty.

That night we camped in the fir woods, on the bank, at the foot of the meadows. Despite a large fire, we again lay pretty cold.

The next morning, shortly after starting off, we saw and fired at a moose that crossed the stream at some distance ahead. The animal ran off at a great pace. As we saw no blood, we did not follow the trail. That day, too, we saw a marten in a pine at a little distance from the stream, but it escaped us ; and we also saw either a large gray fox, or else it was a wolf, cross the river about twenty rods in advance of us.

That night we reached the head of Escohos carry. Here we camped.

We had a hard forenoon's job dragging our load over the carry road next day. It was near eleven o'clock when we passed " Spoff's "

(Mr. Flint's). In consideration of our long hair, coon-skin coats, moccasined feet, and generally dilapidated condition, we had hoped to keep out of sight of Mrs. Flint. But I saw her at a window, laughing, as we toiled past.

"Pete" came out and shook hands with us. We asked if he remembered the "seventy-five cent." Plainly he did.

It seemed good, and odd too, to get out among civilized folks again, where there were houses.

Once more on the ice below the falls we slid on at a good pace. At Spencer's we stopped to leave the axe and settle for the pork, etc., we had taken from the logging-camp. We told him what we had used. Spencer said four dollars. This sum we promised to send him, as soon as we should dispose of our fur; and we did so.

Hurrying on, we left the Magalloway, at its union with the Andro-scoggin, at about four o'clock. We had expected to camp here, but finally concluded to push on to Upton, twelve miles down the Umba-gog. This was far too much for us. We were fearfully tired when, at last, we reached Godwin's, at about nine in the evening. We had come rising twenty-seven miles that day, including the carry road.

They laughed well at our woodsy appearance at the Lake House, — most of all that black-eyed table-girl. But we cared for none of these things.

From Upton to Bethel we hired our property drawn on an ox-sled. Here we left the old bateau.

At Bethel we sold our fur, the whole of it, for a hundred and twenty-six dollars. But as there was here no market for the gum and the fish, we freighted them to Portland by rail; and making up as respectable an outfit as we could from our united wardrobe, sent Fred on with it to dispose of it. The rest of us were really unpresentable.

Fred was gone three days. We awaited his return with consider-able anxiety, passing the time with a relative of Farr living there, and keeping as much secluded as we could.

On the third evening Fred came back. He had sold the trout for seventeen cents per pound, — three hundred and thirteen pounds of it. And for the five hundred and seventy-six pounds of gum he had got two hundred and sixty-four dollars and ninety-six cents, — about forty-six cents per pound.

We received, therefore, for

| | |
|---|---|
| Fur | $126.00 |
| Trout | 53.21 |
| Spruce-gum | 264.96 |
| Total | $444.17 |
| Expenses of the expedition | 46.09 |
| Profit | $398.08 |
| One quarter of this | $99.52 |

Ninety-nine dollars apiece was about what we had, after paying our bills. But we had immediately to buy some clothes, before even going home; so that the sum we actually took home with us was but about eighty-seven dollars.

But eighty-seven dollars went a good way with us in those days. It paid our expenses for nearly three terms at the academy. So, on the whole, we deemed the venture a success.

The old Cannuck muskets and revolver we sold at Bethel, for seventeen dollars for the lot. With this sum the friend who had loaned us the little rifle expressed himself satisfied.

On arriving home, we found our people on the point of sending off an expedition in search of us. It was long before we outgrew the nickname of " The Young Moose-hunters."

Such were our fortunes. We would not confidently recommend a similar trip to any youthful party; yet our well-earned success shows what perseverance will do, with necessity pinching hard.